Sundays

WITH

Millicent

PAMELA DOREEN ROBSON

Typeset in Palatino

Editing, design, typesetting and publishing by UK Book Publishing

www.ukbookpublishing.com

ISBN: 978-1-913179-55-7

Sundays

WITH

Millicent

About the author

For the first three years of my life, I lived in the lighthouse buildings in Corsewall, Stranraer and Port St Mary on the Isle of Man. Then the family moved to live with my grandmother in Newcastle upon Tyne. I was educated at Cragside Primary School and then North Heaton County. The latter being the first school in the Newcastle area to introduce an extra year for pupils to learn further education, namely a secretarial course and an introduction into nursing course. I took the secretarial course and went on to do further qualifications at night school.

I married, had my two children, Karen and Craig, and carried on working part-time in secretarial roles. When the children were old enough, I reverted back to fulltime working for companies in various lines of business, including Northumbria Police and Solicitors. I worked for 20 years for one of the largest law firms in Newcastle, Dickinson Dees, and when the partner I worked for left to set up as a sole practitioner, I went with her. She was a person I very much respected and loved working for her. I worked a further three years there and then retired at the age of 63.

I have now been retired for 10 years and I love every minute of it. I always loved legal work, my employer and the people I worked with, but have never been bored since l retired. I continue to socialise with my friends from work and see them all regularly. I had remarried in 1999 to Alan Robson and we both now spend a lot of our time at our caravan in the Borders, where my father was from and I visit St Abbs often, where my cousin Ann still lives in the Cormack family home. I paint with various mediums and plan to do a lot more canvases in the future, I paint my own Christmas Cards every year and at last, I have written the story of my parents' lives. Something I have wanted to do for years but never seemed to have the time, until now. At this point I would like to thank my brother and his wife for the detailed information they gave me and additional stories to add, and also my husband for taking over all the household tasks while I was engrossed in working my way through pages of notes and typing them all up. It is a story that was too good to be forgotten and I really wanted my children, grandchildren, nieces and nephews and their children to learn all about the history of their ancestors. And I am pretty sure that Millicent and Dennis would have approved.

Foreword

My mother always liked to talk about her past. The family gatherings with her parents, grandparents, aunts and uncles, and the stories she told could have me in stitches. There were also the tales of hard years when her father had to look for work which meant at times moving away from everyone. She came into her own, however, when she talked about my father, Dennis. He was 52 when he passed away, and after that, he was talked about even more. It seemed to keep him alive somehow. How they first met and married was well spoken of, but it was their life in the lighthouse service that really stirred up my imagination. It was incredibly hard. How she coped with a new baby when living on one of the remotest islands in Scotland, I just cannot imagine. Especially bearing in mind that the water amenities only consisted of a cold water tap inside, and rainwater stored outside in a tank for washing etc.

The more she told me, the more I came to realise that I needed to record it all. I encouraged her to write things down herself when she was sitting in her room at the home, and I started taking notes as we chatted, then typing them up.

Her life unfolded in a way only she could tell it. She was the most amazing woman, who tackled things head-on and her determination in all things was evident. She had said from a very young age that she wanted to work with children, even when she was a child herself, and that is exactly what she did.

Her working ethic earned my real admiration as she described how hard the tasks were that she had to endure during her training as a children's nurse, and her sheer determination to look after babies in particular.

When she met my father, it was pure romance, a heart-warming story of how they got together and married. Again, her strength of character was called upon to enable her to face the hardship of living as a lightkeeper's wife during the war in the most remote parts of Scotland. A lesser person might not have risen to the challenge of being torn away from a warm, comfortable house with all amenities on hand, to living on an island in the Firth of Forth, with very few amenities. But she rose to that challenge and took life on the chin.

Things did get easier for her, once they left the lighthouse service, but as you would expect, life never stands still and there were still plenty of challenges to face in the coming years.

When we had these conversations, it was when she lived in a residential home nearby. She had given up her home in Backworth after another spell in hospital and decided that it was time she was looked after, considering she had looked after other people all her life.

I don't know how she managed it, but she out-manoeuvred me so that every Sunday we spent the day together. I would have much preferred to do this on a Saturday for various reasons, but in the end, it worked very well.

I should have known all along that she would have her way. She never liked Sundays in the home because the number of staff on duty was reduced and the meals not quite as good as through the week.

It was the only day she felt like this as the rest of the week there was always something interesting happening. On Tuesdays she was out with Alistair and Edith in the car and was happy to be driven anywhere at all. Other days there were always things going on in the home and she participated in everything, loved the company, the chat, and in particular Michael, one of the carers.

So, Sunday became our day. I would pick her up in the car, to spend the day at my home, sitting in the conservatory. She loved to watch the birds in the garden as they fed and fluffed their feathers in the bird bath. It was relaxing and peaceful. I knew all the things she liked to eat that she didn't get in the home and she happily tucked into her lunch and tea, and sometimes the odd cream cake now and again.

She was so funny because, being a diabetic, she shouldn't have had such things but ate with joy, saying that once a week couldn't harm her. It could be very selective, this condition, because on other days, when she was out with my brother and his wife, she would inform them that she would have to eat soon, otherwise she might 'go into a coma' because of her diabetes. That is rather at odds with her consumption of cream cakes, but age brings an authority of its own, and Millicent was a prime example.

So, Sundays meant we could sit and chat. She was in her late 80s by this time, so really, I knew I should make the most of this time together when she would talk of days gone by. She was always happy to do this, of course, and I was more than happy to listen. I was beginning to find out details of my family history that I had never known before.

It was all really fascinating.

Pamela

Memories

She sat with her coat on, handbag on her knee, waiting. Her fluffy booted toe tapped out her impatience. In front of her was the glass double fronted entrance into the residential home where she lived, and which gave the best view of the car park.

A car pulled in and parked right in front of the door.

"And about time," she muttered.

As her daughter got out of the car and came towards her, Millicent stood up to meet her as she came through the door.

"Now, Mam, don't look at me like that. This is not an appointment, I said I would be here around 10 o'clock and it's only 10 minutes past. Now where shall we go today?"

Somewhat mollified at the prospect of having a 'nice run out in the car' as she would put it to her friends later, the ice melted and she relaxed.

"I fancy a trip to the coast."

And so commenced a routine which had developed over the weeks and was now set in stone. It was Sunday. Pamela would take Millicent for a run in the car, anywhere she fancied on the day. Later, they would have something to eat at Pamela's home in North Walbottle, and then sit together chatting in the conservatory until it was time to go back to the residential home.

Eventually, Millicent would talk about things she had done in the past, before, during and after her life with Dennis. Fate had played many twists and turns in her life, but the main one was how she met him in the first place.

As everything unfolded before her, Pamela soon realised that she needed to keep a record of these stories. It was her family history. Things she had never known before. It was also history in the making of how people lived during the war, which was made even more challenging by the fact that she had lived in the remotest parts of Scotland with only the very basic of facilities.

"You should write it all down, Mam. I can't even imagine how you managed. It's a good job Dad was funny and could make you laugh. Some of the scrapes he got into!"

"He certainly made life interesting."

So began Sundays with Millicent.

MILLICENT OLIVER

Date of Birth: 30th June 1917

Mother: Ellen Oliver (née Ling)
Father: Fred Oliver
Elder Brother: Fred Oliver (junior)

Addresses:
231 Ayton Street, Byker, Newcastle upon Tyne   (until 6 years old)
13 Vane Terrace, Carville, Durham   (until 10)
Neptune Road, Wallsend, Newcastle   (until 12)
1 Alston Avenue, Walker, Newcastle   (until 17)
12 Nidsdale Avenue, Walker, Newcastle
20 Eaglescliffe Drive, Cochrane Park, Newcastle   (until marriage)

After marriage:
Lighthouse Buildings, Inchkeith Island, Leith, Edinburgh
Lighthouse Buildings, Start Point, Start Island, Sanday, Orkney Islands
Lighthouse Buildings, Corsewall, Stranraer, Dumfries and Galloway
Lighthouse Buildings, Port St Mary, Isle of Man

20 Eaglescliffe Drive, Cochrane Park, Newcastle upon Tyne
Four Winds, School Road, Coldingham, Eyemouth, Berwickshire. Scotland
19 Shrewsbury Drive, Backworth, Newcastle upon Tyne
Sovereign Court Care Home, Newbiggin Lane, Newcastle upon Tyne

Chapter 1

There is a saying that 'Saturday's Child Works Hard for a Living' and when Millicent Oliver was born in the summer of 1917 to Nellie and her husband Fred, no-one could ever have imagined just how hard she would indeed have to work, not only for her living, but throughout her married life and beyond.

Her upbringing was a combination of happy family get-togethers, where aunts, uncles and cousins gathered together for an afternoon of eating lovely home baked food, singing around the piano and the telling of funny stories by her uncles. Perhaps it was being amongst so many children, as well as feeling totally at ease in their company, that she grew to realise that this was what she wanted to do in the future. Look after children. It would mean studying hard to be a nurse as well as getting the relevant qualifications in childcare, but that was her ambition. And once Millicent had made such a decision, nothing would stop her working hard to realise that ambition.

She did not have an easy start in life because her parents did not have an easy life, but strong family bonds were built and remained always.

Her father knew what hard work was, being a Plater at Swan Hunter Shipyard in Wallsend, working in all kinds of weather and being physically exhausted at the end of the day. His wife Nellie worked hard too, running the family home, and caring for Millicent and her older brother, also named

Fred. These were the days when the man went out to work and his wife stayed at home. It was her job to make sure there was a meal on the table when her man came home from work, to keep the children away from him while he relaxed, reading the paper by the warm fire she would have prepared and got ready to ensure his every comfort was catered for. As it happened, Nellie was quite happy with her lot. She liked having a home of her own, making it cosy for her and Fred and of course the children. They could be a handful, but she managed them quite nicely too. It would have been easy to threaten any of their misdemeanours with 'wait till your dad gets home', but that was never her way. She dealt with everything herself. She was quiet and unassuming, with an air of silent authority which her offspring knew and instantly regretted if ever they were foolhardy enough to challenge.

The couple had married at 16, and many a critical eyebrow was raised on discovering this information, with a knowing look of 'time will tell why'. It always gave Nellie great pleasure to inform people that No, she wasn't pregnant, just in love. Thereafter, their obvious discomfort was very satisfying to Nellie.

World War 1 was in its third year when Millicent arrived in the world and life was hard for her parents. When it ended in 1918, and shipbuilding waned, her father found himself out of work and he had to think of other ways of earning money to support his young family. He bought the equipment to make ice cream with a view to sell, and at least earn a small income. A complete diversity from work in the shipyard, but it did provide an income of sorts and helped keep the family afloat. A financial disaster was averted one day when a full container curdled, and it was apparent there was no hope of saving the batch of ice cream. However, another well-known local ice cream maker came to Fred's rescue and provided him with the ingredients to keep him going. It was a life saver and he never forgot the hand of kindness shown to him that day. It was still the times of pulling together, when neighbour helped neighbour and survival depended on a helping hand.

The search for work, however, often meant that the family were uprooted from their home and moved to somewhere new. Nellie hated these moves and all that it involved. Packing up all their belongings and leaving the home she had created, and starting all over again wherever her husband had managed to find work. They both had come from large families and often got together in large gatherings, but these could be impossible to take part in if they lived too far away and were missed with a sad acceptance because needs must and it had to be done. One such move resulted in them living in a really remote area in Durham, miles away from their family and friends, which did not go down well with Nellie at all. In fact, it brought out a red-hot rebellious streak in her and she put her foot down once and for all. She was NOT going to live here. They were, as she said, 'living in the middle of nowhere', miles away from both their families, no-one to help them and the house was "no better than a derelict pile of bricks". Normally a quiet and mild-mannered woman, this certainly made an impact on her husband, and Fred promised faithfully he would sort out something better for them.

Nellie's outburst happily brought about the desired result, and they very quickly ended up back in Newcastle in a large, comfortable council house in Walker, within easy reach of almost all of their respective families. And so, peace reigned once more, Nellie was happy, the children were happy, and Fred was relieved to be back working in the shipyards, back with his work friends, doing a job he loved.

As many of his workmates at the shipyard tended to do, he developed a habit of 'acquiring' items which he thought would come in handy for his home or garden. So much so that Nellie once commented, "I am sure I am going to come home one day to find he is building a ship in the back garden". Thankfully, it was a large greenhouse that he built instead, which was much approved of and appreciated by her as it meant that Fred could grow tomatoes and vegetables to supplement the family food supply. He made an excellent job building the greenhouse with proper foundations, eight bricks' height and a firm steel framework for the glass structure. Aye, it was a grand feature in the garden and Fred was very proud indeed, all it needed to complete it was a nameplate and a bottle of champagne to 'launch' it, as with all shipbuilding tradition. It crossed his mind that if ever he was visited at home by his foreman, he may need to keep the curtains closed at the back of the house.

As well as providing all manner of edible produce, it also provided a lovely home for Peter, a large toad that had hopped into the garden one day from the little stream at the bottom of the garden. He tucked himself nicely into the drainage spaces at the bottom of the brick-built beds. And there he lived for many, many years.

There were not many things that Fred could not put his hand to. As well as his work at the shipyard, he also liked to build and create things which would help make their everyday life easier. So once again he got an idea, and this time Fred got it in his head to build a fridge. He drew a plan, combined with a list of things he would need to do the job. This was long before they were commonplace in the home and readily available from the shops to buy. Amongst other things, he needed some copper piping so one day before leaving work, he rolled down his boiler suit and got a friend to wrap some piping around his waist. It was a hard job, bending it safely around his ample middle but eventually it was done, and he pulled up his boiler suit again and prepared to leave for home. The exit from the yard led the workers up a really steep bank and everyone hustled and bustled their way upwards in a great rush towards their transport home. So not only did he have this climb to contend with, it was also a very hot, sunny day too. The weight of the piping and his overheated body added to his struggle, and the extra heat on the bus even more so.

By the time he arrived home, he was absolutely exhausted and overheated. Also, he now had the problem of trying to unbend the pipe and get himself out of the coils. He was most insistent that Nellie had to be careful unwrapping the said pipe because he didn't want it damaged before he could use it. It was a great struggle and Nellie pushed and shoved and tried to ease his rather large framework out of the copper coils. Eventually, and to both their immense relief, Fred was free. He spent the rest of the night recuperating! But build that fridge he did! These were the days of mend or make do, and whatever it took to provide for his family, Fred worked hard to do just that.

One of Millicent's earliest recollections was when she was infected with ringworm on her scalp. A condition almost never heard of these days, but perhaps a sign of the hardship and poor diet of that time. Her mother took drastic action and cut off all her hair so that she could treat it with the special cream she had got from the doctor – breaking everyone's heart in the process because at that time Millicent's hair was long, in thick wavy curls. When young Fred came in from school, he took one look at his sister and said to his mother, "Eeeh, Mam, look what you've done to our Millicent's hair, I'm going to tell me dad on you".

When he came home from work that night and was unceremoniously dragged by his son to look upon his poor daughter, Fred did indeed have a tear in his eye. In an effort to salve poor Millicent's hurt feelings at such a drastic act, and to pacify her husband and son, Nellie bought a pretty mop hat for her to wear until the ringworm cleared up and her hair grew back again. A family photo was taken around this time, depicting Millicent in her mop hat, which on reflection was a bit reckless by someone to consider recording that event in a picture!

Meeting up with family members was a regular and important event in these times of hardship to keep everyone's spirits up. They all regularly met up at her grandparents' house, which was the most central house to where most of them lived. There were many brothers and sisters on both sides of her parents, and thereby many cousins too. Thankfully, quite a few of their relations lived nearby and often a quick walk along two or three streets would often be all you needed to keep in touch. Whoever lived away further than that, prompted arranged visits on particular days. Very few people had cars, so the main source of transportation were buses of course.

If Millicent and family happened to arrive early at her grandparents, she always seemed to be encouraged to go and play with the hens, or to collect any eggs, or to pick some pansies in the garden. She was later to realise the flower picking was to save her grandparents the job of deadheading the plants, which was necessary to produce more flowers, therefore not the treat she initially thought she was being allowed to do. As young as she was, she also came to realise that her grandparents wanted her out of the way so that they could talk to young Fred on his own. They made no secret of the fact that he was their favourite and never showed Millicent any affection at all. This behaviour continued even when everyone was there.

One day, when she was about six, her mother put Millicent on the bus so she could go and visit her grandmother. She knew the stop to get off, and it was a short walk from there to her grandmother's house. When she arrived and knocked on the door, she was brought into the house.

It wasn't long before her grandmother encouraged her as usual to go and see the hens. She did like to see the hens, so out she popped to the hen house, but no-one came with her. In fact, once again, they just ignored her.

After a while, she drew herself up as tall as she could, and went back into the house and said to her grandmother, "I know you don't want me here, so I am going to go and see me Aunt Lizzie". She then walked out of the house and, indeed, went to see her Aunt who lived a short distance away, where she knew she always got a warm welcome and a soothing hug.

How sad that a child as young as she was, was made to feel so unwanted by her own grandparents, that she felt she had to go elsewhere to be welcomed.

There were also much happier times spent at her grandparents' house, however. These were when as many of the family as possible would descend on Neptune Road. Aunts and uncles, and cousins. Aunt Alice would play the piano and everyone would join in a good old sing-song. Then there was a great feast to be had as everyone brought something to put on the table and everyone happily tucked in.

When food had been consumed and it was time to relax as it was digested, Fred senior's two brothers, Norman and Albert, would entertain everyone with their stories of past narrow escapes and disasters. They could spin a good yarn, could the Oliver brothers.

One such tale was when they were trying to impress a couple of girls they had been seeing, long before their marriages of course. Norman had a motorbike and sidecar at the time and the two of them took the girls out for a nice ride in the country. However, Norman, in his enthusiasm to make a favourable impression of his driving skills, shot the bike, sidecar and all passengers right through a hedge and into a farmer's field. They were all deposited in an undignified heap, which did not go down well at all with their female passengers, and certainly put an end to any chance of romance after that.

On a much later trip out with the motorbike and sidecar, but this time with his wife Winnie, Norman was stopped by the police. There had been an accident further up the road, so all traffic was being halted. The officer stayed beside them, chatting and passing the time of day until, eventually, the road ahead was cleared and he moved them on. As they drove away, Winnie gave a huge sigh of relief. Underneath the blanket she had over her knees in the sidecar, she was hiding a side of beef and half a pig. Meat was rationed at the time and at a premium, and Norman was never a one to miss a money-making opportunity.

Norman ended up being the most well off in the family. He had started working down the mines as a boy and ended up managing the mine. He invested in property, bought a shop, ran a pub, amongst other things. He had a brilliant business mind and never missed the chance to make some money. When he and Winnie were out in the car one day (they had moved onwards and upwards from the motorbike and sidecar by this time), he had suddenly slammed on the brakes, put the car into reverse to turn into an area being cleared for demolition. He had spotted men working at an old chip shop and went over to have a look inside. Realising what they were taking out as scrap was better than he had in his own chip shop, he chatted to the men and they came to an agreement whereby they would carefully take out the fixtures and fittings and deliver them to his own shop, for a small fee of course. The men were very happy with this arrangement and of course so was he. He had a keen eye for business, did Norman.

He owned a long terrace of houses in old Washington town, County Durham. He eventually owned pubs in the area. He and Winnie lived in a beautiful large property called Penshaw House, near to Penshaw Monument in Sunderland which was surrounded by large grounds and even had tennis courts. Family meetings there were great fun. He was extremely proud of his new top of the range music system and blasted everyone's ears when he played Bill Hayley's 'Rock Around the Clock' at full volume, which went down very well with the young generation. Not so much with the older ones.

He and Aunt Winnie later had a house built near the sea, between Whitburn and Seaburn, called South Bents. It too was a very impressive building, with huge rooms; the living room in particular had a massive picture window facing the seafront, but best of all, every floor had heated carpets. Something no-one had even heard of. It was sheer joy on a cold day to sit with your shoes off, curling your toes and warming your feet. Everything was the height of luxury with all kitchen gadgets you could ever want and all modern appliances.

They were also one of the first people to own a caravan in what was then a small exclusive caravan site known as Haggerston Castle, near Berwick upon Tweed. The caravan boasted of a bathroom with a full-sized bath and an outside balcony, unheard of in those days, where they would sit and relax in the fresh air and enjoy the lovely views.

At one point, Norman thought he might buy a motorboat. He and Winnie went to the harbour to see a particular boat for sale and he was invited aboard. Winnie declined to join him. The sight of her husband, dressed in his usual trench coat and bowler hat, being physically lifted up by two men and deposited into the boat, sent her into hysterics. She couldn't stop laughing. Whether it was this that was the deciding factor in Norman's decision not to buy the boat was always up for debate and arguments at later family gatherings. The bowler hat he wore was actually referred to as a 'dut', which for some reason made the tale even funnier every time the word was used when regaling the story.

It was said within the family, however, that Norman still had his first pound. In other words, he was known to be 'a bit tight'. Millicent, being an adult at the time and who smoked, asked him one day if he could sell her some cigarettes because she was aware that he always kept supplies to distribute to the pubs. He disappeared from the company then came back with a packet of 10 Woodbines in his hand, saying it didn't matter about the money. She was so shocked at this uncharacteristic gesture of generosity, she said, "I think I should frame them, not smoke them!"

Norman continued throughout his life to be a very shrewd businessman and when he received a letter from the Inland Revenue querying his tax payments, he was adamant that they were wrong in their demands for more money. Correspondence was exchanged and telephone calls made, but an agreement between the two parties was never going to happen. The matter came before the court, and armed with all his paperwork, facts and figures, Norman appeared to present his argument. To everyone's astonishment (apart from those who knew him) Norman proved his point and won his case. There cannot be many individuals who take on the tax man and win, but as his family and friends knew, Norman was no ordinary individual.

Sadly, though, all his wealth could not prevent his beloved Winnie's health problems. She suffered badly from kidney failure. This was long before kidney transplants. Their only son inherited this condition too, so it was just hoped that he would be luckier with the development of better and more effective medical treatment.

During these years of large family gatherings and all the entertaining stories, Millicent's childhood was filled with fun and laughter, but also experience of the hardships that went with her father's occasional unemployment. However, she thrived in this environment and as she grew, came to accept exactly what she had to do to realise her ambition to work with children. To work hard, train as a nurse and obtain the necessary qualifications to do just that.

Memories

"Here's a cup of tea, Mam, did you have a nice nap?"

Millicent was relaxing in the conservatory once more. It was warm and comfortable, and she had nodded off after her lunch. She always liked sitting here but especially in Springtime, watching the birds fighting each other and flying about in and out of the trees.

"I miss my garden," she lamented, "but it's lovely to see the birds again, squabbling as always. D'you hear that racket they are making? We used to call that a 'sparrow's wedding'. They know it is Spring and the males are courting the females. You will soon see their young hopping around the garden in a few weeks' time."

Pamela sat opposite her, notebook in hand.

'So, tell me more about when you were training to be a children's nurse and where you were working. You mentioned the nursery on New Bridge Street and I actually pass that building on my way to work on the bus. I get off at the stop just after it and walk down to the Quayside."

Chapter 2

Millicent threw herself into anything and everything that would develop her knowledge and experience of working with children.

Her Aunt Alice not only played the piano at the family gatherings, she also played the piano at the local Byker Street Mission, and she encouraged Millicent to come too. (*This was where Millicent practised the piano, in the hope that the lessons that her mother insisted on her taking would develop into something reasonably acceptable. But she hated the lessons with a passion and couldn't wait to give them up.*)

She learned that here at the Mission, there was always something going on and something to do. In the main hall there was a billiards table, a table tennis table and a dartboard. Much to her surprise, she discovered she was a dab hand at darts. There was singing and occasionally concerts. On Saturdays, the night always ended up with a dance. Potential light-footed participants stumbled their way around the hall, trying not to step on their partners' toes and with a bit of luck, show how desirable they were to the opposite sex. They lived in hope each week and if a few toes were crunched in the attempt, there was always next week to impress someone else.

Group outings to the coast at Whitley Bay were arranged or a meal at The Jingling Gate in Westerhope. They would catch the tram to wherever took their fancy, hopefully the weather would behave itself for the day, and then they all caught a tram back again.

There were many young people of her age at the Mission, and after the Sunday morning services, a crowd of them would head off to the coast, either Whitley Bay or King Edward's Bay in Tynemouth. Some would cycle there and those who did not have a bike would catch a bus down and then all meet up when they arrived. It was a lovely and cheerful group of people and Millicent was happy to part of it.

She recalled these fun days with great affection. If anyone tried to develop a close relationship with her, they soon realised they were wasting their time; she was just not interested and she told them this. She was focused on her ambition to work with children. She had to study and sit exams. It might have sounded harsh, but it was much better than giving out false hopes and expectations to those with romance in mind. Whenever she did marry, she wanted to be around 25 years old, so there was plenty of time as far as she was concerned.

On top of that, if anyone thought they knew her well enough, and felt confident enough to call her Millie, she soon put them straight on that score too – "My name is Millicent, not Millie". She did not approve of names being shortened.

She got herself involved in the running of the Mission and became a Sunday School teacher there. In for a penny in for a pound, she thought, and became a cub leader too. Camps with the scouts and cubs were both hair-raising and great fun. You had to have eyes in the back of your head at times, just to keep up with whatever they got up to. But it was something she loved doing and the cubs loved her too. When she was 21, the cubs and scouts had a collection and then presented her with a complete set of Disney's Seven Dwarfs. The film Snow White had just been released earlier that year and so the gift was really topical at the time. She loved them and really appreciated the thoughtful gesture from them all.

Also involved in the Scout movement were Lucy and Eppie Averill, who she came to be extremely good friends with. For them, the Scouting world turned out to be a lifelong commitment and they became very well known for their work within the scout movement all their lives.

As their friendship developed, Millicent would visit their family home and spend time there. The Averills were a wealthy family, who lived in the affluent area of Gosforth and Millicent came to know the whole family very well. Their father was a barrister in Newcastle, but she soon realised her friends' mother was a rather strict and starchy matriarch.

Friends of Lucy and Eppie by association sometimes became her friend too. One such friend was a curate, who was considered by Mrs Averill to be a perfect suitor for Lucy and imagined great things for the couple. However, a spanner was put in the works by the man himself, who much preferred Millicent. She liked him, that was true, but only as a friend. When he was obviously trying his best to impress her favourably one day, and knowing her love of wildlife, especially birds, he stood next to the family budgie in its cage, saying "Hello, little dickie bird". Millicent nearly exploded with laughter and any chance of romance flew right out the window.

Not to be put off, however, he continued in his quest to win her over until eventually, having built himself up to do it, he asked her to marry him. Oh dear. Millicent did her best to let him down gently and said she just wanted to keep it a platonic relationship as she still valued his friendship. Later, of course, she did what girls do, she told her friend Lucy. Unfortunately, Lucy told her mother. Mrs Averill was beside herself with anger and made her feelings known to Millicent in no uncertain terms. She was to discover that day that Millicent was no pushover, though, and she stood up to her immediately. Millicent said it wasn't her fault that he had been attracted to her, she had never given him any encouragement, and finally said that she was leaving. It was some months before she went back to her friends' house but eventually she did and happily the dust settled and things were calm once again.

It was during her time at the Mission that she got to know Miss Alice Hands. Miss Hands took Drama, singing practice, and produced and directed the concerts. She was head of the nursery at the Mission too. She was well known as a lecturer at universities on the subject of childcare.

More importantly, Miss Hands also ran a day nursery.

The nursery was funded by Miss Lillian Steele, the daughter of a shipyard owner Steele & Raines. The family lived in the wealthy area of Gosforth and from an allowance provided to her, Miss Steele gave half of it to run the nursery.

Sadly, she was profoundly deaf, but she could lip read and was able to communicate with everyone by some means or other. She was a very formidable and charitable woman and it would have been easy for her to live a life of luxury without the need to work. But children were her passion and she involved herself in anything and everything to do with their upbringing and welfare.

So, under the wings of Miss Hands and Miss Steele, Millicent diligently studied and gleaned every bit of knowledge of nursing and caring for children. She did this training for three years.

She visited nurseries in Elswick, Ryehill and Jesmond, as well as a brand new one in Bensham, Gateshead, which was custom built and had been opened by Lady Astor. Dramatically, the nursery burnt down years later.

Millicent continued her nursery nurse training at Newbridge Street Nursery, just east of Newcastle city centre. It was a square building, with three storeys, and access to the flat roof which had railings around the top for safety.

This was a large nursery, with a Matron, Sister, six nurses and a maid. Here she had to work exceedingly hard, scrubbing everywhere to ensure the best of hygiene and cleanliness. The standards were extraordinarily high, which bode well for her future life and which Millicent strove to upkeep.

When the weather was good, the nurses were tasked with carrying the small babies up to the roof for some fresh air as well as the carry-cots and Moses baskets. Up the steep flights of stairs they would go, baby under one arm, beds under the other. It was a hazardous and terrifying journey for both baby and nurse. How they managed it without dropping a baby was miraculous. The people from today's Health and Safety Standards would have been horrified at such risky practices.

Millicent learned some of life's lessons here too. She thought she worked with friends and happily trusted her colleagues. It wasn't until the Matron took her to one side and told her that one of the nurses had directly blamed her for some misdemeanour that Millicent realised that not everyone was as honest at herself. Matron had known that this particular nurse was guilty of the offence and was kind enough to warn Millicent.

Such were the working experiences all managed by Millicent which set her on the road to success.

Chapter 3

Millicent qualified as a Children's Nurse and passed with flying colours. In her testimonial from the National Society of Day Nurseries, the list of required skills was long and varied, including Organised Play, Infant Care, Management of Children, as well as Laundry Work and Needlework. She used the last particular skill to provide herself with new clothes and hats by making her own. Years later she acquired a sewing machine, which was a revelation and saved her a lot of time when making clothes for herself and other members of the family, not to mention matching hats – which always involved hours of hand stitching when adding beads for special effect.

All of these skills were paramount in setting her apart from the others when applying for the post of a children's nurse. She wanted to be the best at her job and these things helped her to stand out. She was therefore in a good position when applying for work with the best of families requiring help with care for their children.

One of her early employers was a family in Gosforth and there she learned, for the first time, hands-on experience with young babies and toddlers. She was appreciated and encouraged by the parents and soon became confident and efficient in her position. Her strongest recollection of working for this family, however, had nothing to do with childcare. The father in his employment sometimes had to travel to France and on one occasion upon his return, he presented Millicent with a little parcel he had brought back for her. It was a tiny bottle of perfume from Paris. She had gasped with pleasure and was thrilled to receive such a precious thing. And it smelt beautiful. Never had a gift brought anyone so much joy. She couldn't wait to get home to show it to her mother. As she walked home that day, disaster. She dropped the bottle. Horror of horrors. She said she could have wept. She wanted to lie down on the pavement and cover herself with the liquid, before it disappeared down the drain. Telling the tale could still bring that feeling of horror to her, despite the years that had passed.

Her work, of course, would inevitably change as the babies grew up and went on to nursery and subsequently school, and she therefore had to seek work elsewhere.

Her next position was at Eggleston Hall, near Barnard Castle, where Sir William Gray lived with his wife and family. Sir William was a 2nd Baronet and owned the shipbuilding company William Gray & Company, so once again, the shipbuilding world played an important part in her life, considering her father worked in the shipyards for most of his life. This grand property was around 40 miles from where Millicent's family home was and therefore she had to live at Eggleston Hall to be able to carry out her duties. It could have been very daunting for someone as young as Millicent, but she took it all in her stride.

Her duties were to care for his two sons, and attend to their wellbeing during the daytime hours. She would often be seen with the baby in his pram, walking around the grounds of the Hall, taking in the fresh air. She was a very confident young woman by this time.

For some reason, if she was ever referred to as a Nanny, Millicent became very defensive and would immediately correct that to Children's Nurse. It never became clear why it seemed to be an insult, but she certainly made it seem that it was exactly that.

After Eggleston Hall, she went to work for the Lowes family in 1939. They owned a large prestigious store on what was then, and still is, the most important street in Newcastle, Northumberland Street in the City Centre, which was a well-established family business.

That summer, they asked if she would be happy to have a working holiday and go with them to Scotland when they were going for their annual holiday. She would still be looking after the children but of course would have time off for herself.

She happily agreed to do this, having never been to Scotland before, and she really looked forward to going somewhere new.

The house they were renting, 'Ravenscraig', was in a tiny fishing village called St Abbs which was just over the Scottish Border, past Berwick upon Tweed. It was delightfully unspoilt and very picturesque. A row of large houses overlooked the road down to the harbour, which was a hive of activity in and around the harbour walls. There were three sections to the harbour, each with fishing boats of various shapes and sizes anchored in them and a large building which housed the lifeboat.

'Ravenscraig' was one of the large houses in the top row and owned by the Wilson family. It seemingly was what a lot of the villagers did in the summer months: move to a smaller, private part of the property and let out the rest of the house to holiday 'visitors'. It created an extra income on top of their earnings from fishing and proved to be very lucrative.

This visit was to change the course of Millicent's life completely, because it was here that she saw for the first time the man who would steal her heart. Albeit he was engaged to someone else at the time.

She was looking out of the window one day, when this good-looking young man walked past. She asked Mrs Wilson about him and was informed that his name was Dennis Cormack and he lived next door at Ocean View. But, he was engaged to be married. Not to be put off, however, Millicent remembered thinking to herself, 'Hmm, but not married'.

The Cormacks were a well-established family and one of the original families to first live in and develop St Abbs. The head of the family was Tommy, who was an engineer on the lifeboat, his two brothers, Peter and Danny, who were fulltime fishermen in the family's fishing boats and their sister Jeannie. Tommy was a widower who had two sons, Dennis and Jim, and a step-son Bertie. Tommy's wife Annie had died soon after Jim was born, and it was Jeannie who took over the household duties and devoted her life to caring for her three brothers as well as Tommy's young children. Jeannie certainly had her work cut out.

Life can often throw a curve ball at times and as it turned out, things were to change in Dennis's life too, which meant a completely new direction for him and one he could never have dreamt of.

DENNIS WILSON CORMACK

Date of Birth:	13th September 1917
Mother:	Annie Rae
Father:	Thomas Cormack (Tommy)
Brother:	James Rae Cormack (d.o.b. 19th October: 1919)
Step-Brother:	Robert Rae (Annie's son Bertie))
Address:	Ocean View, Briery Law, St Abbs, Eyemouth, Berwickshire. Scotland
Also living at Ocean View:	Tommy's brothers Peter and Danny, and sister Jeannie

In Scotland, married women were often still referred to by their maiden name, hence Annie Rae.

Annie was evidently of strong character and really, quite a brave woman. She was a St Abbs girl and had been regularly seeing a jeweller from Newcastle. When she discovered she was pregnant, she decided for whatever reason, not to marry the father despite his pleas to do so.

It will have been quite a frightening prospect being an unmarried mother in those days, especially in a small village where everyone's private life was common knowledge and such a revelation would be the main topic of conversation. Nevertheless, she held her own counsel, did not marry the father, and in time gave birth to a baby boy whom she named Robert.

Young Bertie, as he came to be known, was still a young child when Annie met and married Thomas Cormack. Tommy worked fulltime as an engineer on the St Abbs Lifeboat and initially after their marriage they lived in Rose Cottage, one of the first dwellings at the entrance to the village. They then moved to Rock House down by the harbour, and later moved into Ocean View to live with his brothers, Peter and Danny and sister Jeannie.

In 1917, Annie and Tommy became the proud parents of Dennis and just over two years later another son, Jim. *(Incidentally, when Dennis was a young baby – he won the local Bonny Baby competition and was presented with a silver spoon with his initials on!)*

Sadly, 18 months after Jim was born, Annie died, leaving Tommy with three young sons to bring up.

His sister Jeannie at this time was engaged to be married, but family ties were strong and she made the huge decision to end her relationship to help bring up the young boys and to run the home for all the family.

Under Jeannie's loving wing, the children thrived and her brothers were well looked after. This she did for the rest of her life until all boys were working adults and married, and they never forgot what she did for them. She had made a great sacrifice, giving up her own future so that they were nurtured and loved.

Young Dennis did cause quite a stir one day when he was doubled up with terrible pain. This went on for some time until eventually the doctor was summonsed and by the time the doctor arrived on his rounds, he was surprised to find Dennis sitting comfortably in the chair, pain-free. He said to the doctor "Och I'm fine now, the pain has stopped", but being pedantic with his patients the doctor asked him to explain in detail where this awful pain had been. As soon as Dennis demonstrated where it had been and how much it had hurt, the doctor acted immediately. He said, "You have a burst appendix, that is why the pain has stopped – we must get you to the hospital NOW." There followed a great flurry of activity getting Dennis into the doctor's car and off they went to the hospital in Berwick where an emergency operation was performed. He was an extremely lucky boy to have survived such a thing that day; others in similar circumstances had not fared so well.

The whole family lived in a large detached house called Ocean View, on Brierylaw, one of the original rows of houses in St Abbs which overlooked the road down to, and beyond, the harbour.

There were more houses dotted around the harbour, one of which was Rock House and it was there that Dennis was born, in the upper bedroom on the right-hand side of the house. The very first occupants of Rock House many years earlier were also part of the Cormack family and when tragically the father died, the mother and her family emigrated to Canada. The contents of the house were brought outside and spread out, and everything was auctioned off to fund the move away from Scotland.

In summer months in more recent times, it became a normal practice by the villagers to let out parts of their homes to holiday makers, and those at Ocean View did likewise. The family left the main part of the house and moved into the annex. There were two separate attic bedrooms, one for Peter and Danny, the other for Jeannie, and in the main living area was a double bed built into the wall and used by Tommy. There was a large black range with a fire for heating and cooking purposes, and a table and chairs in front of the window at the far end of the room. On the back wall were battered but comfortable chairs for them all to relax on at the end of the day.

As the saying goes, though, "there's nowt so funny as folk", and it could have been made for two of the Cormack brothers. Peter could be a particularly argumentative man and he and Tommy had many a falling out over one thing or another until, eventually, they stopped speaking altogether.

Peter's chair was next to the fire in the range, purposely positioned with its back to the bed. When the men ate their meals, Tommy and Danny sat at the table, but Peter sat in his chair to eat his. And this continued for years and years. Now as it happened, all the brothers were extremely good singers with beautiful rich baritone voices and, strangely and somewhat unbelievably, whenever Tommy started to sing, Peter would join in, and vice versa. It was the only time that the two brothers' voices were heard together.

The men like their forefathers before them earned a living from the sea. The Cormack family had owned a large fishing vessel known as a Fifie, named The Alert, and in later years changed to three small fishing boats which were more practical. There was The Whitey which had an Evinrude engine. The locals often referred to the boat as the Evinrude, just because of the name of the engine. When it eventually gave up the ghost and worked no more, the boat was thereafter used mainly as a rowing boat in and around the harbour, or just outside it.

The middle-sized boat was the Dowlaw and was fitted with a paraffin-powered Pettar engine. The boat was so named because Peter and Danny had one day been on Dowlaw Beach further up the coast by Lumsdaine Farm and had collected all manner of wood of various sizes and lengths which had been washed ashore after days of stormy weather. They created a steam tunnel on the beach in which they placed whatever wood they found and steamed each piece into shape and built the boat by hand. Being resourceful folk, nothing was ever wasted which gifted from the sea. When that engine eventually failed, they invested in an outboard engine, which still did the work very nicely.

Incidentally, the area around the beach and the farm was also on the doorstep to Fast Castle, which had been in ruins for centuries. In its time, it had been a huge fortress against intruders and it was rumoured to be the site where Spanish gold was hidden during the Armada. It was said that the treasure was carried by donkeys up Dowlaw Burn, past two waterfalls and up to the original Lumsdaine Farm. The tales of treasure and the 'hidden staircase' at the castle ruins has meant there have been many attempts over the centuries to find the treasure, but alas, without success. Hope lives on.

The largest and most used boat, however, was The Beaver. It had the most powerful engine of them all, a Kelvin twin cylinder engine which was fired up by paraffin and thereafter switched over to petrol. Once out of the relative safety of the harbour, she could power her way through the roughest of sea and was used daily by men collecting the crabs and lobsters from their creels.

It was not an easy life for any of them, bearing in mind the weather played a huge part in what Peter and Danny could earn from their catch. If the weather was stormy and they were unable to put to sea, there would be no income. Thankfully, however, they could always depend on Tommy's wage coming in from the RNLI, which was guaranteed. Probably, the hardest work of all was that done by Jeannie, washing and ironing for four adults and three children (no washing machine in these days) as well as keeping the house clean, and of course preparing food for everyone.

The boys went to the local school in St Abbs and then Coldingham, and eventually Eyemouth. When they left school, all three brothers became lighthouse keepers. As they grew up, of course, they had all learned to work on the boats and to fish as well as emptying and baiting the lobster pots.

Being a very small community, it followed that the boys of a similar age to Dennis and Jim all became good friends. They got up to all sorts of mischief – some of these being documented in a book that their good friend Will Wilson wrote in later years called "Ebb Tide". For instance, when the boys raided the orchard in the grounds to the huge mansion owned by the landowner, which you passed coming into the village. Waiting until the moon went behind the clouds to steal the apples, realising they couldn't see a thing so one bright spark lit a match to look for them. Rather defeating the object. Will was later to become the editor of the Berwickshire News and was very well respected by people in those circles.

A few of the boys got together and formed a band at one stage – called the St Abbs Rocky Mountaineers, with a definite cowboy slant to their music. Dennis, his brother Jim, Sandy Crowe and his brother Freddie, Peter Hood and Will Wilson. They were all good singers and keen musicians, and practised a lot, but most of the time they passed their nights away sitting round a campfire. Occasionally, however, they even played in the village hall for the locals.

The friends regularly met up and went to dances, the pictures and basically anything that was going on, they would be there. Possibly to their utmost disappointment, there was never any alcohol sold in

St Abbs. No pub, not even an off-licence. It had been a strict caveat when the village was built that there was never to be alcohol sold there. And it still stands to this day. Not to be beaten, of course, it was only a half hour's walk to the next village of Coldingham, where a jolly night could be had in the local hostelry called The Anchor.

After the consumption of rather a lot of beer one day, it seemed a good idea to Dennis to have a tattoo put on his forearm. A thistle with 'Scotland' written in a scroll underneath it. And after another night of overindulgence, he had another one put on the other arm. This time a lighthouse – which was his career by this time, a lighthouse keeper. (Millicent stated years later that he would have HAD to have been drunk to have had those tattoos done because he absolutely hated needles.)

Dennis also discovered he had a talent for playing football. In fact, he excelled at it and was in great demand to play for Reston as a fullback. When he was on leave from his lightkeeper duties, someone would immediately commandeer him to play in the next match. He ended up with quite a collection of medals for his efforts. He continued to play football in his adult life, at least for as long as his knees would allow.

Coming from a family who were musical in one way or another, he could often be found in the upstairs parlour at Ocean View, playing the piano or the organ that were housed up there. Many generations of the family would have a go playing them at some time or other. He also was quite adept on the fiddle, which would sometimes go with him when working away. But his favourite musical instrument was his accordion. That went everywhere with him. For years. Every lighthouse. Every home. Before and after marriage. Eventually, after years and years of use, it was in a sorry state, stuck together with patches of sticky tape everywhere, Elastoplast and anything else that would work to keep the air inside, and produce the music outside. It was once deposited in the bin as it was virtually dropping to bits, but it was rescued once more and lovingly restored – with even more sticky tape.

1940

Dennis was stationed on Inchkeith Island in the Firth of Forth, Leith, Edinburgh.

He was engaged to a local girl, living in St Abbs.

Chapter 4

During the holiday in St Abbs, Millicent continued with her duties with the children but in her free time, she walked around St Abbs and the harbour, and the neighbouring village of Coldingham, taking in all the lovely scenery and getting to know the locals. She got to know people of her own age and of course, indirectly, some of Dennis's friends. She learned about the Cormack family living in Ocean View, who were mostly fisherman. The three young brothers, Bertie, Dennis and Jim, were all lighthouse keepers.

She was also introduced to Dr MacDonald and his wife Marion who lived in Coldingham, as well as John and Isabelle Walker who owned Coldingham's butcher's shop. She was invited to tea to both households, and lifelong friendships began.

When the holiday ended, the Lowes family and Millicent said their goodbyes to their new friends and returned to Newcastle.

Millicent kept in touch with John and Isabelle Walker, and the following year went to stay with them for her annual holiday. They lived in Applyn Cross in Coldingham with their young son David.

Whilst walking around the village one day, Millicent bumped into Freddy Crowe from St Abbs who she had got to know the previous year. They chatted for a while and then he informed her, with a twinkle in his eye, that Dennis had recently been jilted by his fiancée. In fact, he had been due to marry that weekend. It transpired that whenever he was on leave, Dennis developed his social life with his pals, as well as being commandeered to play football for Reston at every opportunity, resulting in his fiancée feeling neglected and forgotten. She had therefore found someone else.

He had been devastated at the breakdown of the relationship. When he was returning to his duty as lighthouse keeper on Inchkeith Island in the Firth of Forth, his kneejerk reaction was to throw the engagement and wedding rings in the river on the way over there.

Freddy went on to tell her that a gang of them had arranged to go to the pictures in Eyemouth that night, and did she want to go?

Of course she did.

They picked her up from Applyn Cross in Dod Brown's bus and off they all went. It must have been Freddy's mission to get Dennis and Millicent together because when they returned to Coldingham afterwards, Dennis was pushed off the bus with her, and told to make sure she got home safely, and off the bus went.

It was laughable because the house was just across the road from where they were standing.

They went inside and shared cups of tea with John and Isobel. Tactfully, they then put their young son to bed and left the couple on their own. Dennis asked her if she had been up to St Abbs Head, where the lighthouse was. She answered that she hadn't, so he arranged to take her the next day. They said goodnight and he then set off on the two mile walk back to St Abbs, while Millicent went inside to give details of her night out to the very excited Walkers.

The following morning, Dennis arrived at the house and was sat chatting to John as he waited for Millicent. Little David, who was four at the time, suddenly piped up with "Have you been here all night?" Millicent instantly turned pink! He had seen Dennis the previous night, before he had gone to bed and this morning, as far as he was concerned, he was still there!

The couple set off for St Abbs from Coldingham and walked through the village on the way to the lighthouse. She realised she was 'on show' as they passed through the streets and was later to discover that she and Dennis had actually walked past the house where his ex-fiancée lived. He obviously wanted people to know that he could get someone else too. Millicent could tell that he was still upset at the turn of events, but he did his best to be cheery and good company.

They walked from St Abbs up the coastal path which went past a lovely little bay called Starney. The way Dennis talked about the bay made her realise it was obviously a very special place that meant a lot to him and his family. Each generation had been taken there as a child and it was very dear in their hearts. In the Spring the banks were laden with the palest of primroses and the flowers hopefully signalled the beginning of a warm summer. They would pick small bunches of the pretty little flowers and take them home for all to enjoy. It was also where children went every Easter to 'roll' their hardboiled eggs, in a traditional race from the top of the bank to the bottom, to see whose could last the longest before the shells fell to pieces. It was great fun. Starney was a place she was to revisit on many occasions in the future.

Eventually they arrived at the lighthouse and the views were breath-taking. At least the keepers here didn't have to climb up a steep tower to attend to the lens of the beacon, because you actually went down steps to the small tower there. Being on such a high cliff top was evidently high enough.

The cliffs were also home to thousands and thousands of sea birds of all varieties. Cormorants, gannets, guillemots, and kittiwakes to mention a few. And the noise was deafening! At times the couple had to shout to be heard over the collective cries of the birds.

Dennis began to relax and was actually very good company. He was funny, and attentive, and Millicent was a captive audience. He had a sparkle in his green eyes, which seemed to ignite a sparkle in hers too. There was also that dimple in his chin – which she found rather alluring.

He told her about his work as a lighthouse keeper on Inchkeith Island in the Firth of Forth, near Edinburgh and Leith. Quite often, being a keeper meant living an isolated life, in remote coastal areas with only fellow keepers for company. Sometimes it could be a lighthouse tower in the middle of the sea.

At least here, the island was currently occupied by sailors and soldiers also working on the island during these war years, keeping watch over the whole area. She realised you had to have a special kind of temperament to do his kind of work, considering the keepers who were stationed together would have to be easy to get on with, because if they were posted on a lighthouse in the middle of the sea, they would have to get on. One grumpy keeper would be unbearable. She came to the conclusion that Dennis was perfect for this job, he was so nice, with a happy outlook on life. And she liked him very much, the more time she spent with him.

Sadly, all things come to an end and eventually the holiday was over and Millicent once again returned to Newcastle. She continued her work with children, and wondered if a certain Scotsman was thinking about her. She worked hard and as the months passed, looked forward to the next time she could travel north.

It was July the following year before Millicent once again had the opportunity to stay with the Walker family.

She told them that she was sure Dennis had forgotten her, but as luck would have it, he was on leave at the same time as she was on holiday. Fate smiled upon them and eventually they met each other once more in the village and again they went for walks together and even managed a few dances too.

She later learned that when she and Dennis had walked around St Abbs and the harbour, his family had been watching them through their binoculars. They were obviously keen to see what this new interest in Dennis's life was like and if she was going to meet with their approval.

August bank holiday arrived and once more she was back in Coldingham. Dennis was on leave and he started to meet up with Millicent on a regular basis. They spent a lot of time together and by the end of the weekend, they arranged to keep in touch and write to each other. This was quite a commitment for both of them, Dennis moving on from his broken engagement and the fact that Millicent was actually romantically interested in someone was huge. Her life had been filled with possibilities and opportunities, but she had just not been interested – until now. She realised this man must be pretty special to be having such an effect on her.

Progress had been slow, but at least it now was actually progressing!

By December, the couple had continued to write and got to know each other a little better. She was invited to stay with John and Isobel for the New Year and she was more than happy to accept, with the added bonus it coincided with Dennis being on leave for a whole week.

Auld Year's Night as it is known in Scotland was a very memorable one for the couple. Talks were had, happy warm feelings expressed, and on 3rd January 1942 they announced they were engaged to be married. Millicent was given the Cormack ring of seed pearls and amethysts. It was such a happy and long-awaited time. The couple adored each other and it showed.

Millicent and Dennis arranged to meet her family and they set off to catch buses firstly to Berwick, and then on to Newcastle. Their very good friend Will Wilson was the editor of the Berwickshire News at the time in Berwick, so they all met up in the town centre and after a quick cup of tea, he wished the couple good luck and waved them off on the bus.

Dennis met Nellie and Pa Oliver, and her brother Fred – who had just become a new father. His wife Elsie was in Gilsland Nursing Home and had given birth to a baby boy on 3rd January. Dennis was such a hit, they named the baby after him. As the baby grew up, he was, as often happens in similar naming circumstances, thereafter known as 'young Dennis'.

Eventually, at the end of his week's leave, Dennis returned to Inchkeith to continue his duties. It had been an eventful week, full of comings and goings, celebrations and meetings.

All of it wonderful.

Chapter 5

I t was a full six weeks before Millicent saw Dennis again. He only had a
24-hour pass, but they were so keen to see each other, Millicent said she
would travel up to Inchkeith to see him there. They did not want to waste
precious time by him travelling to see her.

Easter 1942

Millicent travelled up to St Abbs and this time she would stay overnight
for the first time at Ocean View with the Cormack family, to break up her
journey. That night she chatted with everyone and told them all about
herself and her family and they in turn told funny stories of what Dennis
and his brothers used to get up to as they were growing up. She was
discovering just what a mischievous character her new fiancé was.

The following morning, Tommy made sure she caught the train to
Edinburgh and Dennis had asked his good friend John Wells to meet her
at Waverley Station. John was also living on the island. He was in the Army
and had been stationed there. He had experienced what they called Shell
Shock back then, and he had developed a bad stammer because of it. He
was a very companionable soul and was the perfect person to put Millicent
at ease on this their first meeting.

Dennis had described him to her and added that she should look out for the sun shining on his golden hair – which turned out to actually be his bald head. And she did actually recognise him, despite the humorous description.

John proved to be good company and Millicent liked him immediately. He was a very well-educated man and well spoken. They got on extremely well and when he took to calling her Millie, for some inexplicable reason, this was acceptable to her. Perhaps it was the way he said it that won her over. Even so, he was the only person who was ever allowed to call her that. Things didn't change that much!

They travelled together to Leith Docks and caught the War Department boat which would take them over to the island. She had been provided with the necessary special pass to enable her to enter the Docks, and another pass to land on the island. Being war time, personal identity papers were essential and constantly checked wherever you travelled.

It was a 30-minute journey over to Inchkeith and, fortunately, the weather was fine and therefore no choppy sea to contend with on this, her first trip over there. The boat was full of servicemen who were either returning from leave, or starting their posting. There were sailors and soldiers, as well as a group of show people from E.N.S.A.

E.N.S.A stands for Entertainments National Service Association and had been established in 1939 by Basil Dean and Leslie Hanson to provide entertainment for the military during World War Two. Apparently, every Sunday, a show took place on Inchkeith for everyone living on the island, so that was something to look forward to.

In the distance, Millicent could see the shape of the island and it grew in size, the nearer they got. The lighthouse tower was right on the top of the highest point and she could vaguely make out quite a lot of other buildings too. It was an incredible sight.

Inchkeith Island had a history going right back to Napoleonic days, with many different stories to tell. From experimental isolation, a place where plague ridden people lived until they died and were buried there, and then, a line of defence against the enemy during various wars. All around the base of the cliffs were rolls of barbed wire, huge concrete blocks to prevent unwanted landings, and scattered at various points over the island were huge guns. There were high tower buildings acting as look-out points to every direction and because of the army and navy personnel living there, a lot of accommodation buildings. There seemed to be a building at every twist and turn for either military purposes, or for the day-to-day running of everyday life. (*There were no Royal Air Force personnel living there as they were stationed on another island.*)

The boat approached the harbour wall and turned into the safety of the inner jetty, and everyone disembarked. Dennis was there on the pier to meet Millicent and John, and together they began the walk up to the lighthouse buildings. The steep bank was known to all and sundry as Heartbreak Hill, which Millicent thought was a very apt name, as they puffed and panted their way up.

When they reached the top, they passed a row of houses on the right-hand side. This was where the military officers lived with their families. Ahead of them they could see rows and rows of huts where the servicemen lived, and beyond those, the lighthouse buildings with the tower right in the middle of them. Apparently there used to be tennis courts where the huts now stood, which was a shame because tennis was one of the few sports that Millicent quite liked playing. Such was life during the war years.

They approached the lighthouse and there waiting to greet them were the Assistant Keeper, Eddie Black, his wife Mary and their daughter – who was known for some reason as 'Winkie'. She was four years old and apparently even at that tender age, she was well known for mimicking the people in the ENSA concerts. Millicent was to stay with the family for the night and they made her feel very welcome.

During her stay, she was introduced to the Quartermaster, known as 'Timber' Wood, who was later to play a part in the marriage of Millicent and Dennis. He owned a jeweller's shop in Edinburgh and in his time there on leave, he made their wedding ring.

That evening, Millicent and Dennis joined those who were off duty to watch the show being put on by ENSA. She said later she thought it was wonderful and very entertaining. These shows did exactly what they were intended to do, they brought moments of lightness during the dark days of war and helped the servicemen deal with the day-to-day stresses of life during those troubled times.

The following morning, sadly, Dennis was back on duty and it was time for Millicent to leave the island. She returned to St Abbs to spend another few days with the family and then she caught the train back to Newcastle.

Chapter 6

Tommy Names the Day

I t was a few days later when Millicent received a letter from Dennis. It transpired that his father Tommy had telephoned him to suggest why not get married on the 25th July. Tommy had worked out that this was the only day that all three brothers would be on leave at the same time. (Bertie was going to be on a week's leave and Jim would be too but expected to go back on duty in Fair Isle the following day.)

The couple had discussed when they would like to marry, of course, and had planned it for the following summer, in 1943. *Dennis had said he thought that a Christmas wedding would be nice, but Millicent was quick to inform him that he could have one then if he wanted to, but she wasn't going to marry anyone in the winter. So that suggestion was discounted as quickly as it had been voiced.*

So, in an air of excitement, they thought why not? Time seemed very precious in those days and years of uncertainty and neither of them wanted to waste a minute of it. Tommy had named the day, and July 25th it would be.

The decision was made, but it meant there were only six weeks to arrange it all. There followed thereafter a great flurry of activity, there was such a lot of work to do. It was war time, of course – could they really bring it all together in such a short space of time?

Millicent booked St Michael's Church in Byker for the ceremony and then a room at the Co-op on Newgate Street in Newcastle city centre for the reception. She 'bribed' them to extend the number of guests allowed at the reception from 30 to 50 (although she never explained how she managed to do so).

She had a choice of two wedding dresses, but no choice of flowers. It was roses or nothing.

She borrowed a veil from her mother's friend, Cissie Dinning.

Uncle Norman got icing sugar for the cake by exchanging sugar from Dennis's ration allowance.

Her friend Lucy was to be bridesmaid and as luck would have it, she had her own pretty lilac embroidered dress that would be ideal for the day. Her bouquet of pink roses complemented the dress beautifully. Millicent's bouquet was made up of red roses, with sprigs of white heather for good luck.

John Walker, in his usual comical manner, also provided her with some white heather on the day of the wedding. Some to wear in her hair during the daytime he said, and the rest in her 'goonie' at night. So typical of John – but it did tickle Millicent's sense of humour very much.

Miraculously, everything came together in time for the big day, and everyone breathed a huge sigh of relief. The venue booked, invitations sent and acknowledged, cake made and wedding attire ready to go.

25th July 1942

So, on this day, Millicent Oliver married a very special man, her Scotsman named Dennis Wilson Cormack.

As someone stated on the day "and the bride was radiant".

And she was.

The photographer took as many photos outside the church as he could of the couple and the family and friends. In one of the photos, you might even spot a small pottery rabbit which Lucy had grabbed from the hearth of Millicent's home at Eaglescliffe Drive before they left. At that time, the family had a pet duck called Horace, and for one worrying moment, Millicent wondered if she had brought him too. Luckily, she hadn't and subsequently, poor Horace missed his chance in the limelight.

Millicent met Dennis' brother Bertie, wife Meg and young son Robert for the very first time at the wedding reception after the ceremony, so sadly they never made it onto any of the wedding photos.

Dennis and Jim were very similar looking, same height and build, even their hair, and there were a few occasions during the day when Millicent would walk up to him from behind and make the mistake of linking arms with him instead of her new husband. They were both in their uniform, so it was an easy mistake to make, but a few giggles would always follow.

When the Reception was just about over, Dennis, Jim and their friend Will Wilson walked up on the stage, and proceeded to serenade Millicent with a very special song. They were in fine voice that day and harmonised to perfection as they performed "Be Nobody's Darling but Mine".

Be Nobody's darling but mine love
Be honest, be faithful, be kind
And promise me that you will always
Be nobody's darling but mine

They were all very good singers and not a wrong note was had. It was a particularly lovely and moving moment, and the room was filled with emotion. When they finished, the applause rang round the room from an appreciative audience, and not least of all by the bride.

Then it was time to go. The couple bade farewell to their families and friends, and set off for a short honeymoon in a little town called Rothbury in Northumberland. They had booked the weekend at a boarding house there for some peace and quiet before starting their married life. It was a lovely place, and was always remembered as being a very special time spent there.

They returned to Newcastle to deal with the task of cutting up and sending out portions of wedding cake. Dennis had recently met and made friends with the manager of Lees Bakery who had sent a large piece of wedding cake as a wedding present. This meant they were able to send their many friends and family a portion of cake. Something rare in this time of war. The top layer of their own wedding cake, together with the remains of the extra cake was packed up and taken with them to St Abbs and Inchkeith, to apportion to family and friends there.

Once again, all their belongings were packed up and the family waved them off at Newcastle Central Station on their way to St Abbs. They would spend some time there before once more heading to Dennis' work at the lighthouse. When they arrived at Ocean View, the family greeted them and another reception awaited them. The Scots know how to celebrate and a villager's wedding was the perfect excuse for a party – if indeed they needed an excuse. Millicent and Dennis were then inducted in the traditional ceremony of what is known as being 'creeled'. This ceremony was a great tradition in fishing villages and towns, and most certainly by the people of St Abbs.

This is where a new groom is tied to a creel with ribbon, and the bride has to cut him free – with a blunt knife.

A local man known as Wal carried out this ceremony with them and his reward was cash and whisky. Not a bad day's work, was it?

The next day, Millicent and Dennis left St Abbs and caught the train once more to Edinburgh. Thereafter, they made their way to Leith, where they caught the boat which would take them over to Inchkeith Island.

What a huge step this must have been for Millicent. She was used to working for well off families in beautiful homes with everything you could possibly need to make life easier, as well as living at her own home with her parents which was quite a new build and was very modern. She was on her way to a completely new way of life. She knew from her short stay on the island that no 'mod cons' were waiting for her there, everything was very basic and still rather behind the times. She must have loved him very much to leave the world she knew behind her and take on a much harder way of living.

It was both exciting, exhilarating and terrifying. But with Dennis by her side all the way, she looked forward to new and exciting times together.

Of course, everyone on the island was aware that the boat would be bringing the young resident lighthouse keeper and his new bride, and had prepared to welcome them in style.

INCHKEITH ISLAND
Firth of Forth
Edinburgh

PRINCIPAL KEEPER:
Mr Thompson
(Mrs Thompson and two sons)

1ˢᵗ ASSISTANT KEEPER:
Mr Eddie Black
(Mrs Mary Black and daughter Agnes – known as "Winky")

SUPERNUMERARY KEEPER:
Donald Maclean
(from Scalpay Island)

(Plus Occasional Keepers)

Army Officers and Soldiers
Naval Officers and Sailors
Marines

Chapter 7

Inchkeith Island, Firth of Forth

The boat slowed down and turned into calmer water alongside the inner pier which was one long structure reaching out from the land. Where the pier met the land, it continued over to the right towards a small pebbly beach and a smaller, lower pier where presumably smaller craft were landed.

Millicent could see once more the road leading up Heartbreak Hill to the very top of the island where the main living quarters of the servicemen were and of course the lighthouse buildings, her new home.

They all disembarked and there ahead of them, lined up along the pier, were rows of servicemen all standing to attention. Soldiers and sailors were awaiting the arrival of the young resident lighthouse keeper and his new bride, and to welcome them to their new life on the island.

Also there on the pier, the naval tractor was waiting. Dennis noted that it now had a trailer attached to the rear of it. As they walked up to the tractor, they could see a seat on top of the trailer, which turned out to be a double seat from an old bus, and spread over the top of it, were two flags – one was the Union Jack and the other the Saltire, the flag of Scotland.

This was to be special transport which had been created especially for the new bride and groom. It was hilarious – if not rather precarious, considering how steep the road ahead was. Would they be able to make the journey up there without sliding off?

They had to clamber up onto the trailer and once aboard, sat side by side on the double seat, and hung on for dear life as the tractor moved off.

The journey up Heartbreak Hill was fraught with worry as the tractor chugged ever upwards. It was doubly worrying because Dennis was quite aware that the driver, Tubby, had already put two tractors over the cliff and into the sea.

As the procession progressed, they passed more servicemen on the way up the road and each and every one of them stood to attention and saluted as they went by.

It was truly a lovely and remarkable welcome.

Another warm welcome awaited them at the lighthouse buildings where the Principal Keeper's wife, Mrs Thompson, had arranged yet another reception for the newlyweds. Some army and naval personnel had been invited too, including of course John Wells. Millicent was full of emotion as she joined the group of cheerful people inside and a good time was had by all. It was a daunting prospect, starting a brand-new life in a really remote place with this man she loved so much, surrounded by servicemen who were ready to fight to defend this island from the enemy. A huge change from what she knew as a children's nurse in a large city in family homes.

But for an initial start to all this, a party was just what the doctor ordered.

Their married quarters turned out to be a flat on the ground floor to the right of the tower, and Millicent proceeded to make it a real home for the two of them. It was going to be a challenge to adjust to the lack of amenities and things that she took for granted. For instance, there was no running hot water, just a cold water tap indoors. All water had to be boiled for drinking and for washing etc. Worst of all, the toilet was outside. All very well in the warm summer months, but a bit of a challenge in the winter.

Added to this, washing had to be carried to an outdoor wash house which was through an archway at the side of the building. There was a big iron 'set pot' which had to be filled with water and a fire lit beneath it to heat the water up before she could wash anything. There was a large porcelain sink to the side, where she could rinse it all through, again by hand.

Past the wash house and up a few steps was a small green, which was the delegated drying area for the lighthouse personnel. The original drying area now had naval huts built on it, so there wasn't much space left to hang out any washing.

It was hard work. Again, so different from what she knew. But she got on with her tasks and the first time she hung out her washing, she was sent a poem from one of the servicemen called Guy Preston entitled 'The Lightkeeper's Washing'.

On Inchkeith I've a cabin and the view from it is free
Of the Lighthouse Keeper's laundry and beyond that lies the sea
And when a ship's approaching, I can follow its advance
By the trail of smoke appearing o'er the Lighthouse Keeper's pants.
On Inchkeith I've a cabin and I overlook the Forth
The famous bridge confronts me on a bearing West by North
But alas, I never see it, though I peer for all my life
For its hidden by the bloomers of the Lighthouse Keeper's wife.
The Rodney and the Nelson, the Victorious as well
All pass beneath my window, can I see them? Can I hell.
They are ships on which the Germans would love to shower their bombs
But I view them through a camouflage of brassieres and combs.

Millicent thought it was hilarious and was something she treasured. So much so, she kept it always.

As the months passed, Millicent adjusted well to life on the island, although she did say there was very little privacy.

There were sailors living in the rows of huts in front of the lighthouse buildings, as well as soldiers working all around the building and in the look-out posts next to them. Further out on the island, of course, there were look-out points in every direction and huge guns everywhere.

There was a nice garden at the back of the lighthouse, which was quite steep, but was no problem to the goats that were kept there.

There were cats everywhere. 'Breeding like rabbits' was how Millicent described it. They lived under the huts and in holes in the ground all over. There was a huge tom cat, who was the daddy of them all. Every now and again, the servicemen would have to cull those who were very old or ill.

The soldiers gave Millicent a kitten one day, but she didn't dare touch it for weeks because it was so wild. Eventually, the little thing did eventually tame down and it was a lovely pet. She said it was the sailors who had it spoilt!

On the whole, the weather on the island was lovely, even in December.

The food for all the servicemen on the island was prepared by the Navy, Army and Air Force Institute, otherwise known as N.A.A.F.I. and there were always three or four chefs at any given time. When Millicent and Dennis were invited to eat there, she said the food was always beautiful.

When the keepers received their servicemen rations, they gave them to the chefs, who would make all sorts of treats for them, shortbread, cakes etc., which was a real luxury during the war.

Sometimes the sailors would catch some lobsters and crabs, and the chefs would cook and serve the dishes up at the next dance.

When E.N.S.A. put shows on, the couple would always try and go because it really was good entertainment and an escape from everyday life.

Christmas and New Year were particularly good times socially.

The Army held dances on a Saturday afternoon, once a fortnight, which Millicent said were great. A.T.S. girls were shipped across with their officers, and Wrens too. The dances were always early, around 5pm, because they all had to be taken ashore again one hour before sunset by the War Department boat.

Chapter 8

As the months passed, Millicent threw herself into daily life alongside Dennis carrying out his work duties. Keepers worked on a basis of two months' work and one month off on leave. For that one month off, they would go to stay with their respective families, both at St Abbs and in Newcastle, and for those four weeks at least, they could both enjoy modern conditions again, which made them realise how good it could be as opposed to the hardships on the island. They would shop in town for whatever was needed at the time, socialise with friends and catch up with everyone since the last time they had seen them. They also managed a visit to the cinema whenever they could. It was good to re-charge their batteries before going back to Inchkeith.

She gradually got to know some of the people living on the island, which was good for the soul. She liked people and was interested in them. And they liked her. Being a military stronghold on an island, there were very few females for the men to chat to and for just a few minutes during a conversation, it was nice to hear a feminine voice for a change.

She had already met 'Timber' Wood on her first visit to the island and of course he had made her wedding ring. It was nice to see him again and thank him once again.

With so many people living in close proximity to the lighthouse buildings, it could have been rather overwhelming, but Millicent had always mixed well and was used to socialising with large groups, so she took it in her stride really. It was good to learn about them and what their life had been before being enlisted in the Forces. Wartime meant that a change of direction was thrust upon them. Whatever their dreams and ambitions in life were, fighting for their country took priority and they had to face up to the fact that whenever it ended, it was possible that they had missed the chance to realise those dreams and ambitions.

A regular visitor to the couple's home whenever he was off duty was, of course, their friend John Wells. He and Dennis had a good rapport and often had Millicent in fits of giggles. She could see why they were such good friends; they had the same daft sense of humour.

One of the sailors, a man known as Ginger Reid (*which may have had something to do with his mop of bright auburn hair*), apparently thought that Millicent's name just did not suit her. Quite a brave statement if ever there was one. He told her she looked more like a 'Christine'. Once he had tested the water and had not been shot down in flames, he called her that name for the rest of her stay on Inchkeith. Secretly, she seemed to like the idea of having a different name. At least he had not been foolhardy enough to call her Millie!

There were other visitors to the lighthouse, who came to use the facility of the telephone. They were permitted to make calls to their loved ones, with strict time limits, of course. This was a great luxury during the war and would be pre-arranged because not everyone at home had their own telephone. It proved invaluable to the wellbeing of the servicemen to be able to touch base and reassure their family, as well as themselves, that all was well.

Gradually, on a Sunday, there developed a weekly gathering of servicemen who would join Dennis in their home whereupon a game of cards was enjoyed.

Now this did not meet with the approval of Millicent at all. In fact, it is fair to say that she resented these meetings with a passion. She had been brought up in a strict family environment when Sundays were revered and restricted in pastimes. There was no such thing as 'popping to the shop' to make even the smallest purchase. Father would not have allowed it.

So, there was a great rumble of resentment building up in the Cormack household.

Things eventually came to a head when, one evening, she was asked to make the numbers up and fill in for an absent player.

Now was her chance.

She stood tall, looked directly at the men and firmly declined their kind invitation, saying as firmly as she could, "I do not approve of gambling on a Sunday, and especially in my own home, and there is no way I would even consider joining your game."

There immediately followed a stunned silence and the little group quietly and humbly disbanded. Dennis would come to learn that his new wife was a force to be reckoned with if there was something she felt strongly about. Not for her was the quiet little woman behind the man.

The following day, Millicent received gifts from the men by way of an apology, and which was greatly appreciated. Bacon and Mars Bars and the sweet taste of success.

And there was no more gambling on the Sabbath.

In the spring of 1943, Millicent happily discovered she was pregnant, which as she said "made life interesting".

As soon as the Army doctor heard the news, he arranged for her to get fresh milk from the NAAFI canteen on the island. This was a real luxury, considering they usually had tinned milk.

The doctor in Leith told her she should get off the island before she was five months gone, but she managed to stay on a bit longer. However, as time went on, she was finding it increasingly difficult to make the walk up Heartbreak Hill whenever she returned from the mainland.

Her own doctor in Newcastle, Dr Willie Gibson, had arranged for her to go to Gilsland Nursing Home in Northumberland to have her baby, where her little nephew Dennis had been born. Dr Gibson was also a family friend and had been instrumental in Millicent's decision to go into nursing and encouraged her with her studies. He even gave her one of his medical books.

Eventually, after another uphill climb, Millicent accepted it was time to go to her parents' home in Newcastle to await her baby's arrival.

Before leaving, she said goodbye to the other wives at the lighthouse, the people she had made friends with and John Wells. She would be missed by them all. Finally, she sadly said goodbye to Dennis, who was still working. It was the first time they would have been apart since being married. He would manage on his own until they would be reunited as a family.

She travelled back to Eaglescliffe Drive in Newcastle and settled in with her parents and enjoyed once again the luxuries of modern amenities. It was good to be home.

Her mother Nellie and friend Doreen Sutherland who lived over the road, organised a treat for them all, a trip to the pictures to see a film called 'The Life and Death of Colonel Blimp'. They had heard a lot about it and looked forward to seeing it very much. However, all hopes of a pleasant evening at the picture house were dashed when it was that day that the baby decided to arrive. And in a hurry. There was no time to go to Gilsland as planned.

Doreen was there at the birth, which was a difficult one and it was necessary to use forceps. (*When it was all over and everything was well, Doreen commented that she thought that they were going to pull the baby's head off at one point!*)

Dr Gibson took a photo of the baby, to add to his collection. He had photos of every baby he had delivered. He pinned them to a curtain in his surgery and said it was a good way to keep his records up to date.

And Millicent was delivered of a baby boy.

Alistair Thomas Cormack. Born 20th September 1943.

He was humorously known for a quite a while thereafter as 'Colonel Blimp', due to his unexpected arrival on the day of the planned visit to the pictures.

While all this was happening, Dennis had received orders to "Pack effects ready for transfer" and on the very day Alistair was born, he travelled up to Start Point lighthouse on Sanday Island in the Orkney Isles. This journey took in all, three days, and there was no means of communication during that time.

He did not know until he arrived at the lighthouse at Start Point and received a message on the two-way radio that Millicent had had the baby. A son. He was thrilled to bits!

And yes, he did 'wet the baby's head' in celebration later.

START POINT LIGHTHOUSE
Start Point Island
Sanday
Off North Ronaldsay
ORKNEY

PRINCIPAL KEEPER:
Mr Alex Campbell
Mrs Susan Campbell *(known as Susie)*

CROFTERS ON START ISLAND:
Wallace Family:
Bill Wallace
Lizzie Wallace
Children: Rita, Billy
Lizzie's brother – Georgie (Geordie)
Lizzie's Uncle – Wullie

CROFTERS ON SANDAY ISLAND:
Thompson Family:
John Thompson
Lizzie Thompson
Children: Lesley (son), Mary

Moodie Family

Bill Wallace's Sister and Brother

Anna May

Chapter 9

It was a full eight weeks before Dennis got to meet his son. He had travelled down from the Orkney Islands to Newcastle, which was another journey taking three days by boat, train and bus, but at last the little family was reunited.

The baby's christening was all organised. Her friend Lucy was to be Godmother and John Wells the Godfather. On the morning of the ceremony, John and Dennis' pal from St Abbs, Will Wilson, insisted on dressing the baby. As Millicent said, neither of them had a clue, adding that Dennis was clueless as well.

Thankfully, little baby Alistair, albeit in a rather ruffled state, was ready for the big event, and they all made it to the church on time.

There was then the prospect of the three-day journey back to the Orkney Islands, which Millicent said was a nightmare because there was a new baby and all the paraphernalia that went with him. It was with great relief to all parties that they arranged the journey so that it would be broken up by staying with friends and family on the way.

A taxi took them from home to Newcastle Central Station, they caught the train up to Berwick and were collected by friends who took them to St Abbs for a short stay over. Dennis' family got to meet the new member and it was of course a good excuse to 'wet the baby's head' (again).

Jeannie thoroughly approved of his name, especially the middle one, and said, "There's aye been a Thomas in the family."

The next day for the threesome, it was a matter of up and ready to catch a lift to Berwick once more and off to Edinburgh on the train. The train to Stirling left Edinburgh around 6.30 and once there, they had an hour's wait for the next train. They changed again at Inverness. The train after this was a slow, overnight train which would get them into Thurso around 11.00am the next day. At least on this one, there was time to relax and to catch up on some sleep, taking it in turns to care for baby Alistair.

Throughout all these journeys, Millicent had to manage to feed the baby in as much privacy as her surroundings would allow. She had made a specially designed dress with a front frill, which protected her dignity during feeds. However, she came to learn that the four servicemen travelling with them at the same time on one of the trains showed her the utmost respect and consideration by turning the lights off to ensure she had that privacy.

As the train pulled into Thurso Station, there waiting on the platform for them was Dennis' brother Bertie. He had recently been posted to Duncansby Head lighthouse, which was one of the most northerly lighthouses situated at the tip of Scotland. Visitors were few and far between for keepers living in remote places, so when Dennis had been posted to the Orkney Islands, Bertie knew the family would be travelling nearby on the way. His and Meg's invitation to stay with them and their young son Robert for a few days was gratefully accepted by the couple and everyone looked forward to spending some time together.

Millicent said they had three lovely days with the family before the next stage of their long journey.

When it was time to continue their travels, Bertie drove them to Scrabster where they were to catch the steamer 'St Ola' and which would take them to Stromness in Orkney.

This meant crossing the Pentland Firth. And what a journey that was!

The sea was rough and tossed the steamer around as it made its way to their destination. Millicent was sea-sick, the baby was sick on Dennis, another keeper's wife who was travelling on the boat with them was also sea-sick. Millicent said later that it was three hours of torture.

So, it was a rather bedraggled group who thankfully disembarked at Stromness. The family then had to catch a bus to Kirkwall, along with the Moses basket and luggage and find their digs which had been booked for an overnight stay.

When they arrived at the address, the folk weren't expecting them. Their son had completely forgotten to tell them of the booking. But they were lovely people and once the initial mix up was sorted, they made a meal for them and made them feel very welcome.

A bedroom was prepared and they lit a fire in it to make it cosy. However, the fire hadn't been lit for years and smoke quickly filled the room. The chimney flap had been closed to keep the draught out and forgotten about. So rather than the smoke from the fire going up the chimney, it was filling the bedroom.

The windows were thrown open and Dennis managed to re-open the flap before everyone passed out.

To their relief, the rest of their stay passed without further complications.

Bright and early at 6 o'clock the next morning they ate a hearty breakfast, bade farewell to their lovely hosts and caught the boat which would take them around the islands. They landed at Kettletoft on Sunday at 1.30pm.

There was no public transport or taxis here. You had to depend on local businesses and islanders lucky enough to own a car for a lift. Today, it was Mr Sinclair the butcher who picked them up. He chatted away to the couple and even took them to his home, where he prepared a lovely hot meal and cups of tea for them. It was the sort of hospitality that was unknown in cities, but exactly the sort of thing done in small communities.

The tide was going to be in for a few hours which prevented the couple travelling on from this little hamlet as this last part of their journey involved them walking over the causeway to Start Point Island, where the lighthouse awaited them. So, they spent a few hours chatting to Mr Sinclair, about his life on the island and enquired if he lived on his own. He replied, "Och, my wife died a few years ago. She was in hospital with gallstones but I wouldn't agree to an operation to remove them. I dinna believe in operations."

Millicent was appalled. Being a nurse and having knowledge of modern medical procedures, she couldn't believe what she was hearing. She couldn't keep quiet about it either, and told him that her father had had that operation eight years ago and was today fit and well. She was shocked that such a kindly and helpful man could be so set in his ways that he could stand back and allow his wife to die when she could so easily have been saved. She would learn that islanders had their own opinions of life and living, and were not easily persuaded otherwise.

The area between the two islands was known as the Sound of Sanday and once the tide was out, you could easily walk across the causeway to Start Island and up to the lighthouse. As they learned in time, you could still manage to walk even when the tide was in, albeit you needed waders to do it. A simpler and dryer method was in a small rowing boat.

Time passed by, the sea flowed outwards, and the causeway was revealed. The couple thanked Mr Sinclair for his kindness and prepared for the final stage of their journey. They eventually reached the road end with all their belongings. They put the Moses basket on the pram with the luggage, Millicent carried the baby very carefully as the tide was still going out, and Dennis managed the rest with help from Bill Wallace. Bill was a crofter on Start Point Island, and had come across to help the family get up to the lighthouse. He was quite used to assisting new keepers with all their goods and chattels and made it his business to find out when someone new was arriving. It was a huge help. It was quite a walk and by the time they reached the lighthouse they were all exhausted.

All in all, it had taken three taxies, three lifts, five trains, two buses, one boat, and finally, a few hundred-yards' walk to cover the journey. Three days of travelling with a new baby and luggage. No wonder they were worn out.

The Principal Keeper had just changed and so it was the newly appointed Alex Campbell and his wife Susie who greeted the weary travellers. Susie had prepared a lovely tea for them all which was so welcome.

Thereafter, a lifelong friendship developed between the Cormacks and the Campbells and after life in the service ended, they kept in touch with each other. Many years later and long after Alex had died, Millicent and Dennis holidayed in Invergordon with their family and went to visit Susie who lived locally. She persuaded them to take her on 'a wee run' to see some mutual friends who were still in the service. The wee run turned out to be the other side of the country!

It was Susie who gifted three Cairngorm rings to Millicent in thanks for a great friendship and she wore them regularly. These were later distributed to her grand-daughters Karen and Susan, and grandson Iain's wife Barbara.

During all these stages of the journey, Millicent had stoically attended to Alistair's every need, feeding, changing clothes and nappies and, as she said later, all in all, they had managed everything very well.

Their life in the lighthouse service once again proceeded into a new routine. Dennis recommenced his daily duties and Millicent set about to make their married quarters homely and comfortable.

If life at Inchkeith had been a challenge, it was nothing compared to Start Point. There was still a tap for cold water inside and a large tank within the grounds to collect the rainwater. The tank was completely lined with slates, to prevent leakage and keep the water as cool as possible. If it didn't rain, the water had to be rationed.

There were only Elsan toilets, which had to be regularly manually cleared away and they were yards away from the living quarters, down by the perimeter wall near the main gates, and so was the wash-house.

The wash-house had a large boiler inside, and a fire underneath to heat the water. No washing machines here! There was a tub on a wooden bench, with a cork to release the water when washing was finished. Each family was designated a particular day to carry out their washing. Millicent and Dennis's washday was a Thursday. Millicent said they had great fun when they washed their blankets, as they would both jump up and down over them, spilling the soapsuds everywhere.

Again, if it had not rained, washing would have to wait until it had.

It was a completely different situation compared with life on Inchkeith. There were no longer large groups of servicemen for a start. There was the Principal Keeper and his wife and themselves, and as this was just a small island, only one croft at the far end, near the crossing at the 'Sound' to Sanday.

The lighthouse tower was an impressive sight, with black and white vertical stripes, which was extremely unusual.

She thought Start Island was a bit "niffy", as she put it, particularly at night when the tide was out. The whole area seemed barren and bare. Not one tree grew on it anywhere.

There weren't even rabbits living there, just a few sheep and cows, and one very old horse. There were, however, lots of birds. On one of the beaches, there was a half ship on its side, which brought shelter and nesting opportunities for the birds.

As with most Lighthouse properties, there was a walled garden for the keepers to grow their own produce and keep poultry if desired. There were healthy rows of vegetables, and a small chicken compound with a hen-house. At least they would have eggs too.

As the season moved through autumn, they settled in for the winter. The nights were extremely long in Orkney and as they were one of the most northerly of the islands, daylight was in short supply and could be as short as only two to three hours. It was November by the time Millicent arrived there; Dennis had been there for six weeks, so had had time to get used to it. Although she did say that the weather wasn't as bad as she had imagined, certainly not as cold. She said they only had two showers of snow the whole time they lived there.

It must have been another great challenge for Millicent, having to cope with practically no facilities in the way of hot water and just a cold tap, outside toilets and rationing food until their supplies were brought over, and having to raise a young baby. She found a great support, however, from Susie Campbell, the Principal keeper's wife. The couple had no children of their own and so made a great fuss of Alistair. She would tell Millicent and Dennis if there was going to be a dance at the RAF base and offer to babysit for them. Of course, a decision was made without too much debate and the couple would accept at the drop of a hat. It wasn't very often these dances occurred, but they would always go if they could manage it.

If the tide happened to be in on these occasions, they would wear waders to cross the Sound as it wasn't too deep, or they would borrow the rowing boat. Once across, they would walk all the way to the dance – there were still no buses or taxis there.

There were a quite few crofts on the island of Sanday. These were mainly stone built cottages where families lived and worked small landholdings. The people living in the cottages were known as crofters. And crofters knew how to have fun as well as working hard on the land. Celebration do's and dances were always well attended, and the younger family members in their 20s would also be keen to go, wearing of course their 'party' dresses. It was certainly different from dances in the cities, but nevertheless, their enthusiasm was tangible. These were times to let their hair down, forget the quiet island life, forget war-time restrictions, and make the most of the music, the dance and the company.

Millicent learned at the first dance that she had to be very careful what she said or did when in company with the islanders. She only ever drank lime and lemonade, always. As she made her way down some steps onto the makeshift dancefloor, she stumbled and was helped to balance by Dennis. They continued on to the floor and danced around with gusto. It was the last dance before everyone disbanded and made their way home in various directions.

The next day when Dennis went to meet the grocer's van, he heard that it was being said that Millicent had fallen down when she was drunk at the dance! He laughed at that and told the grocer that he had been dancing with her and she had certainly not been drunk, she only ever had soft drinks. He left the grocer to continue his spread of the news, hopefully with the truth this time.

On another occasion, when the district nurse came to check over baby Alistair, she told Millicent that some of the crofters had been talking about her being cruel because she put her baby outside in his pram throughout the day and left him. Millicent was once more horrified that she was being talked about, especially about the care of her baby – he was only outside during the short daylight hours, to sleep in the fresh air and she kept an eye on him the whole time. The nurse reassured her that she had set the record straight on that score, saying he would be a lot tougher than their babies who were kept indoors in front of the fire all winter. Millicent said she just had to laugh it off and let them get used to her.

Chapter 10

Despite the little tales and tittle-tattle, Millicent came to learn that the crofters were actually very kind people and notably, to her and her husband. If the couple decided to go for a walk over to Sanday, they would be quickly spotted and invited in for tea. There were treats of pancakes, scones, or whatever had been baked that day. One crofter even had boiled some eggs especially, in anticipation of them walking by. You had to remember that during war times when fresh food was in short supply, the keeping of hens was common to assist in food provisions, so such a treat was often as a personal sacrifice to the islanders.

It was inevitable that being the only people living on Start Island apart from those at the lighthouse, the Wallace family were the first ones Millicent and Dennis got to know well. They had met Bill, of course, when they had first arrived. There was his wife Lizzie, their two children Rita and Billy, as well as Lizzie's brother Georgie and her Uncle Wullie. And they all lived together in the croft near the Sound of Sanday, next to the causeway.

It was a very primitive building, made with rough stones, some of which were off the beach. There was no plaster on the walls inside, and there were tiny windows. The ceiling was extremely low and you had to duck your head down as you stepped inside.

In the winter months, the house was effectively halved, whereby a dividing wall was erected using bricks of peat, which had been manually dug out of the ground with a specially shaped spade. Their livestock lived on one side of the wall and the family on the other. As the months passed, and the peat was used on the fire to heat the house, the wall would reduce, and the animals became a lot more visible. It was not a particularly clean environment. But that was the way it was.

Lizzie's brother Geordie was sadly both deaf and dumb. He and their Uncle Wullie worked together on the farm, sharing the work between them. Wullie had listened with amazement to Millicent's story of their long journey from Newcastle to Start Island. He had heard about trains but had never seen one in his life. He was fascinated at how many times she had travelled on them from such a long way away in England.

Little Billy was a rascal and was always up to mischief. His sister Rita was evidently not blessed with good looks, or as Millicent described her to Dennis, she "had a face like the back of a bus". Whenever a dance or some 'do' was arranged, Millicent would make it her mission to help Rita look prettier by applying some of her own makeup and even lend her a dress to wear. Nature sometimes needed a helping hand.

Millicent thought the girl was a 'right tough child'. This was proved right when she had visited Millicent at the lighthouse one day. As they were chatting, she mentioned to Rita the problem they had with their rooster because it was particularly vicious and would charge at anyone who dared venture into its enclosure near the hens. Collecting eggs in particular was getting more and more risky. It had once chased Millicent right across the hen run. Rita asked if Millicent had a sack, which she was then provided with, and into the hen house she went. There followed a right old scuffle, loud clucking and feathers flying, then Rita emerged from the hen house with the rooster in the sack. Millicent was in awe because she certainly wouldn't have tackled that particular job. Rita went home with the offending bird still in the sack and swopped it for a much milder one, much to the relief of Millicent, and peace was restored once more in the henhouse.

Millicent said they were a really friendly family and guests were invited on a Sunday. She came to realise that Lizzie always prepared things in advance of these visits. The inside area was washed in Jeyes Fluid – which unfortunately would be completely overpowering to the eyes and lungs of the visitors. They were hardworking but not the cleanest of people, in fact she wondered if they ever washed. They made their own butter 'from the coos' so anything offered to them that was buttered, was eaten with great trepidation. She did wonder if the churns were ever washed. In compete contrast, the table was always set with beautiful linen, which was obviously Lizzie's pride and joy.

Over on Sanday, Bill's sister and brother lived in a croft about three or four miles along the shoreline. Millicent and Dennis would also visit them when invited. Much care was taken when having tea with them, however, because the food could sometimes be rather challenging. On one particular visit, some home-made doughnuts had been freshly made and offered to the couple. This was going to be a real treat. Or so they thought. Not only did they look a bit suspect, but it turned out that they were also as hard as rocks. The couple stoically soldiered on, voicing their appreciation and pocketing the offensive delights at the first opportunity. When it was time to leave, they were handed a bag of even more doughnuts by the kind crofters.

On their way home along the sands, Millicent and Dennis had great fun flinging the doughnuts across the surface of the sea and counting how many times they bounced before they sank beneath the waves. They did hope that they stayed down on the seabed and didn't surprise them by floating back on the tide because they really didn't want to hurt their hosts' feelings, no matter how bad their baking was.

When a Halloween Party was planned to take place in a barn on Sanday, the couple were invited to this special event. Susie was delighted at the opportunity to babysit Alistair, and off they went to join in the fun. As soon as they arrived, they were given a plateful of what was known as 'Clapshot'. This was mashed potato, turnip, cream and butter, all beaten together, then lucky charms and silver threepenny pieces mixed in too. Millicent said you had to take care when eating, but added that it tasted really lovely.

After the food, the children would entertain everyone. Some were very good indeed. One young boy, aged around nine or ten, was supposed to recite a poem. His mother, who knew the poem off pat, stood beside him, prompting him at each turn. If he stumbled over the words, he got a thump in the ribs each time. The poor boy was in tears, but Ma kept on to the bitter end. Millicent said it was a long poem too! They all had a great time and everyone came together and joined in the entertainment.

Rita Wallace was there that night too, wearing Millicent's frilly pink dress and a 'poke bonnet' which she had made for her. As she said later to Dennis "she did her best, poor lass" referring to her lack of good looks.

Once in a while there would be a dance in the small hall on Sanday. As always, Susie was happy to babysit Alistair, and off the couple would go. It was quite some event, always to be remembered for various reasons. Millicent was asked to dance by a chap who still had his work boots on – and he worked on a farm! She accepted, of course, so as not to offend him, so it was with some trepidation that they set off on the dancefloor. Amazingly, those big and hardworking boots danced around without stepping on her toes once, much to her relief. And another social event that passed with only good memories.

These gatherings were so important to lighten the harsh reality of living in the Orkneys in the winter especially. Millicent didn't like the long dark nights and said it took some getting used to. She would be cooking their lunch when daylight was breaking at 11.30am. Then it would be dark again by 2pm. The oil lamps were seldom off throughout the winter.

During these dark nights, she would try out different recipes, some delicious and welcomed by Dennis, others not so much. He never knew what would be waiting for him when he had finished his day's work. His sense of humour often saved the day when faced with something of an experiment to tickle his taste buds.

As well as cooking and baking, Millicent found that knitting was both relaxing and practical, creating clothing for not only baby Alistair, but also herself and Dennis. Plus, she always purchased the wool locally, which was beneficial to the small local shop. It passed the time away and she was never bored. She commented that she never had time to be bored, there was always something to do if you thought about it.

The fresh food in winter tended to be a bit odd. So much depended on the weather around the islands. If the boats were unable to put to sea, there were no supplies carried to the islanders. The meat was always fresh but for some reason the vegetables were poor to buy. It was for this reason that the keepers would turn over the soil in the walled garden by the lighthouse tower and grow fresh vegetables there. All manner of seeds and young plants were purchased and enthusiastically planted in neat rows and keenly watched as the months passed. It certainly was a successful venture that everyone benefited from in time.

When Spring arrived, Millicent said it was wonderful, and so fascinating. All the different birds that lived on Start Island would be nesting. She and Dennis had to be really careful when walking on the pebbly beach because quite a few small wading birds had their eggs amongst them and were difficult to see.

Ducks nested all over the island. They never moved off their nests. You could put your hands underneath them to see if the eggs were hatching and they would just sit still.

Otters were often seen in the sea too. Millicent would take Alistair to see them playing in the water.

Summertime was lovely and most welcome. It was light for most of the 24 hours. It would perhaps be dusk for a couple of hours during the night. At 2 o'clock in the morning, however, it was possible to clearly see over to Fair Isle, and that was miles away. At midnight, if you felt so inclined, you could sit outside and read a newspaper. The light summer evenings were also when the couple would go on their walks around the islands and visit the crofters.

Anna May's little croft was one of Millicent's favourite places to visit. It was a long walk across Sanday to where she had a little shop in one of her rooms and sold, amongst other items, things she had hand knitted herself. When the couple had first arrived on the island with their new baby, she had sent a 'wee woollen bunnet' for Alistair. They had called soon after to thank her and realised she was a very interesting lady with an amazing imagination.

As soon as they stepped into her living room, they were astonished at what greeted their eyes. Every wall, and even the ceiling, had been completely decorated with the contents of wallpaper sample books. Various shapes and a multitude of designs in various colours were everywhere. Anna May was extremely proud of her unusual but highly original décor. Millicent said it was like a lovely patchwork quilt. The couple expressed their admiration to Anna May, who explained that she had done it all with lovely books from Edinburgh.

The croft was always spotlessly clean, with floors of smooth rock. Despite the flooring, the home was always warm and welcoming to anyone who called.

Millicent always enjoyed their visits there.

Many years later after the war, the women's magazine 'Women's Weekly' published an article about Anna May and her unusual décor, combined with photos of the impressive patchwork walls and ceiling, and she was quite a celebrity for a time.

Ellen (Nellie) and Fred

Nursery training for a young Millicent on the right

Family photo – with Millicent and Fred Jnr (Note the mop hat)

Millicent working at Eggleston Hall, with the children of Sir William Gray

The Walkers

The Cormack Family (L to R) Danny, Tommy, mother Elizabeth (seated), Peter and Jeanie

Dennis in his Northern Lighthouse Service uniform

The wedding – notice the rabbit from the fireside hearth

*(L to R) Tommy, Jeanie, Jim, Dennis, Millicent, Lucy, Nellie and Fred
(note blurred Jeanie laughing – poked in the back by Jim!)*

Approaching Inchkeith Island

Start Point Lighthouse, Sanday, Orkney Islands

Susie Campbell and Millicent with baby Alistair

Corsewall Lighthouse, Stranraer

A tattered but treasured photo of the Chicken Rock Lighthouse, Isle of Man

After a flight between Newcastle and the Isle of Man
– evidently a rough passage for poor Alistair

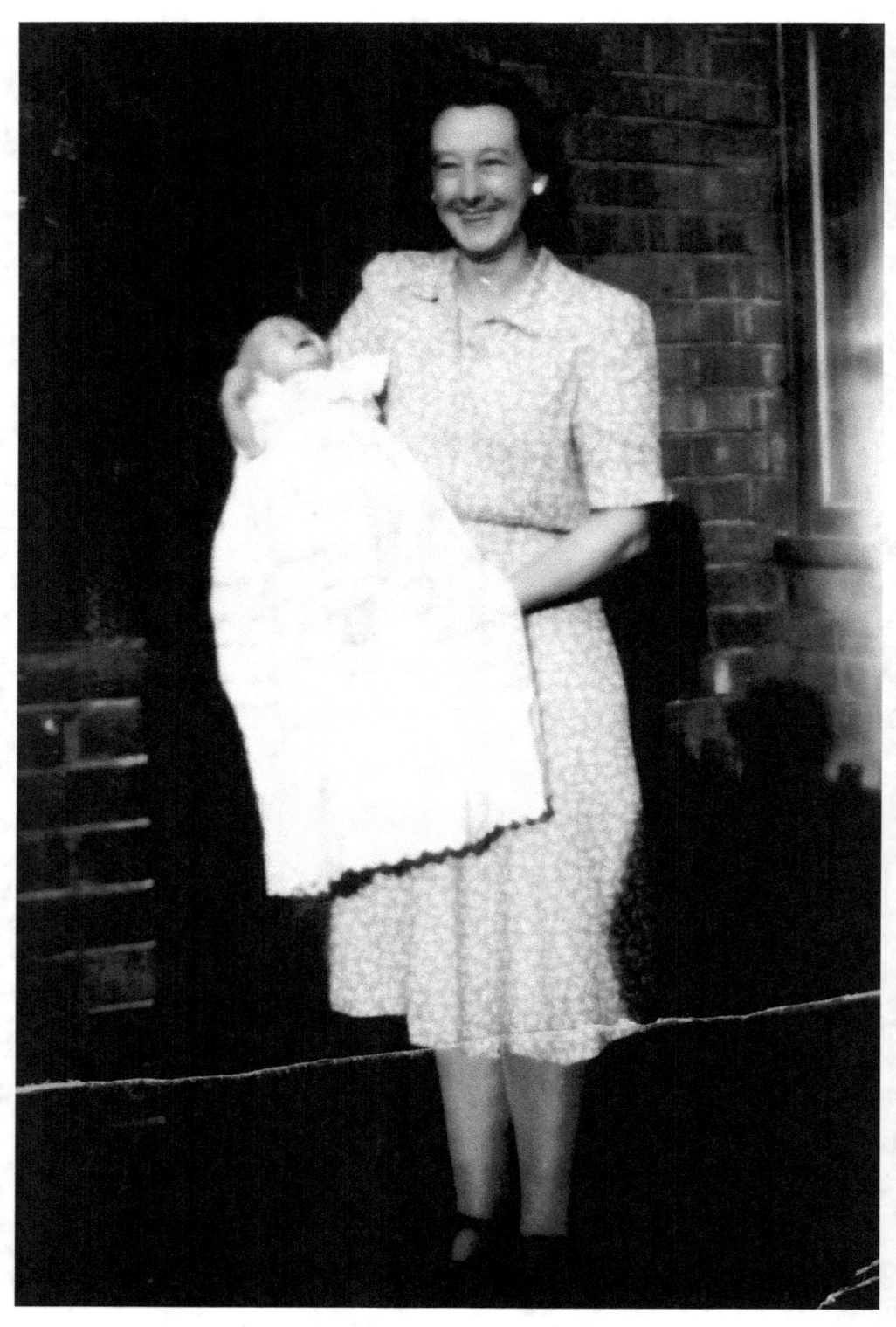

Godmother 'Aunty Sutherland' with baby Pamela

Nellie, Millicent and Dennis outside Eaglescliffe Drive, Newcastle

Bertie (half-brother to Dennis and Jim) Robert and Meg

1942 - 1967

Millicent & Denis

invite you to

A Social Evening

on Tuesday 25th July, at 7.0 p.m.

in the

Tenants Hall, High Heaton

R. S. V. P. to 20 Eaglescliffe Drive,
Newcastle-upon-Tyne, 7

Invitation to the Social Evening to celebrate Millicent and Dennis'
silver wedding anniversary.

Dennis in full voice – with his beloved accordion

Dennis with his trophy for catching the First Salmon of the Season – presented to him by the Duke of Northumberland (photo taken at work on nightshift, hence him looking a tad tired)

Millicent's home at Four Winds, Coldingham

Millicent at home at Shrewsbury Drive, Backworth, Newcastle

Millicent at Susan & Simon's wedding – supporting her team in the FA Cup Final (despite the groom's support of Man United)

Millicent

The Family

Dennis and brother Jim on Inchkeith
– circa 1940.

Pamela on Inchkeith in 2018

The Thistle and the Rose, together on the River Coquet, Warkworth

Alistair and family

Pamela and family

On Inchkeith Island in 2018 – Karen, Pamela, Alan and Craig

Chapter 11

The war was occasionally brought very close to those living on the Orkney Islands. One such time was when a sea mine was spotted floating on the tide and drifting slowly towards the coastline of Start Island. With each tide, it floated nearer the land and then back out again.

For three days and nights, everyone held their breath and hoped that the tide would eventually take it right out to sea. Those living nearby were all warned to stay away from the area. By the fourth day, it was still there and it was obvious that it would need to be blown up, otherwise it could be doing just that where people could be killed.

The decision was made to contact the military, who would attend and get some target practice in to boot. The bomb disposal personnel attended and fired at the spikes of the bomb. They aimed to damage one of the spikes, which would send acid down into the inner section where the explosives were, and then the whole thing would explode. And explode it did! The noise was deafening and the sea shot into the sky and all around it, but at least everyone was safe.

Sadly, a keeper and his wife living on Fair Isle weren't so lucky. During a German bombing raid, the lighthouse buildings were hit and they were killed. The authorities decided that all lighthouse keepers should be trained and provided with Lewis Guns. Dennis attended the Gunners School at Stromness where he was taught how to use the machine and when he returned home, the Lewis Gun was there waiting for him. And it was quite some machine! It was a gas operated machine gun, with a 47 round drum magazine. It might have been a reassuring thing to know you were in possession of such a weapon to defend yourself with, but it must have been a daunting thought for Dennis that he might have to use it one day – a thought that he didn't like to dwell on.

Lizzie's uncle, Old Wullie, caused a right stir one day at the lighthouse. It was a daily occurrence for people living on the islands to scour the beaches for anything of interest, or value, which they could use or sell. There were all kinds of flotsam and jetsam to be found along the waterline and amongst it, things from ships or vessels which had sadly been sunk during the war. A block of rubber, for example, when handed to the authorities, could be worth a week's wages. It could be quite a lucrative pastime, strolling along the beach during these times.

Wullie had called in to see Dennis this particular day and looked forward to the usual offer of a cup of tea. As they sat supping and chatting, Wullie said, "Oh Dennis, I found this on the way here this morning, what do you think it is? Do you think it might be worth anything?" and produced to Dennis what was a live incendiary device! Dennis nearly choked on his tea, jumped up and exclaimed, "Dear god, Wullie! Get the hell oot o here with that bloody thing, it's as good as a bomb" and Wullie was unceremoniously shoved out of the house with his find. The offending item was later blown up on the beach, and Dennis's blood pressure returned to normal.

Another day, it was Bill who had a great find. He and his young son Billy had been, like everyone else, walking along the beach, checking for anything of interest that they could utilise. In the distance he spotted what appeared to be an oil drum. This was a really good find. Oil was hard to come by, expensive, and always useful. He hurried over and with great effort, rolled it up the beach to safety from the incoming tide. Billy meanwhile was idling around on the waterline to see if he could find anything for himself.

Bill decided to puncture the drum to check the contents. Unfortunately for Bill, it wasn't an oil drum. It was a smoke bomb. These drums were used out at sea by naval vessels when being pursued by the enemy and they would be jettisoned from the stern of the ship over the sea, and upon submersion into the water would explode, thus creating a huge smokescreen around the ship for protection.

It had exactly the same effect on land. The whole area disappeared in the smoke. A magician couldn't have done a better job of making the island vanish. And where was little Billy? He had vanished too. So, picture the scene: nothing to be seen except thick grey smoke, and a frantic voice shouting *"B I l l e y"* .... *"B I l l e y"* .... *"Where are you, B i l l ey"*. Bill was desperate to find his son and it was a good while before the smoke gradually thinned. But eventually it cleared and young Billy appeared through the mist and was reunited with his father.

It was a deflated Bill who returned home that day. The two of them were in a right state from all the smoke and he didn't even have the oil he thought he had found. Aye, life could be disappointing at times.

Life went on as normal for everyone else and, over time, Alistair was growing more adventurous around the lighthouse buildings. Because the whole area was surrounded by a boundary wall, it was normally a safe environment for him. However, when he was still just a toddler, he went missing. He had developed a love for collecting eggs from the henhouse next to the walled garden. He had everyone in a right old spin when his absence was noticed. They all searched far and wide, and he was eventually seen in a field on the other side of the henhouse. He had discovered how to open the little gate between it and the field, and had gone exploring. His visits thereafter were more closely monitored, and Millicent's heart rate eventually managed to calm down.

On one of their walks, Millicent and Dennis would sometimes call in to see Mr and Mrs Moody, crofters living on Sanday. They lived just past Anna May's croft. Millicent liked visiting this clean and friendly family. They would be asked to "Tak tea?" or "Tak cheese?" and were offered fresh bread and cheese. The cheese was made by the family and was delicious. Millicent had seen where the cheese was prepared and it was spotless, which was very reassuring.

The toilet facilities were, however, a bit of a challenge. When Millicent was shown where it was, she was taken up a path at the back of the house, to a barn next to the cows, and the toilet was actually in the cow byre. Island life was certainly an education at times.

The couple had a daughter who was married with two little girls and Millicent got to know them quite well. She once gave a hair slide to the elder daughter, something which was obviously loved and treasured. When later asked who had given her the slide, she would look at Millicent and shyly say "Bonny Maggie". And the name stuck all the time they lived there.

Millicent built up good friendships with the crofters and their families. They were so diverse and interesting. In return, they also got to know the lighthouse keeper's wife and came to confide in her and treat her like a friend.

One day when visiting Maggie Thompson, the wife of crofter Jimmy, they sat chatting over a cup of tea as normal. The couple had a son and a daughter and Maggie mentioned that her little girl's coat needed washing but because it was pure wool, she couldn't bring herself to do it in case it shrank. Millicent offered to wash it for her, promising that she would be extremely careful as it was something she had done before in her training.

Millicent took it back home and gently washed it in mild, soapy water. Care was taken in drying it flat, to keep its shape and it was perfect. The colours were, once more, cleaner and brighter. When she took it back, Maggie was thrilled with the result and relieved that, indeed, it was as good as new.

Another Thompson family living on the island were Lizzy and John Thompson and their son Lesley and daughter Mary. Millicent couldn't remember if they were related to Maggie and Jimmy.

The longer they lived here, the more families they came to know, each and every one of them being unique in their own way, but always so kind and friendly to the keeper and his wife. Despite the daily hardships of running their home at the lighthouse, the friendships of these people certainly lightened their load.

When Dennis had leave due, they decided to have a nice break and go to Newcastle to visit the family. It was like returning to the modern world, where luxuries could be as simple as having hot and cold water – in a tap! They would always make the most of these visits and meet up with as many of their friends as possible. When it was time to return to Orkney, it was again a challenging trip but over time they had got used to it.

One year after such a visit, as they were heading back along the road to the lighthouse, a really strange and unbelievable sight met them. They had to stop walking to look more closely. A huge green and moving mass covered the area. It was up the walls around the lighthouse, up the lighthouse tower, the lighthouse buildings and over the ground, like a slow moving carpet.

As they got closer, they could see that there were millions of green caterpillars crawling everywhere and over everything.

Alex had been completely overwhelmed by the whole event and had been anxiously awaiting Dennis' return so they could tackle it together. He and Susie had managed to clear them from inside their living quarters, but outside they were still everywhere in sight. He and Dennis had to get cracking and try to get rid of them somehow. Millicent said they had got into their flat and were on the furniture and curtains. The two men decided to spray everywhere, clearing the walls, the lighthouse tower and all the surrounding buildings of the tiny creatures. Finally, they had to sweep them all up and dispose of them. It was exhausting work.

It was days before they were cleared of them. The poor garden looked awful, there wasn't a green leaf in sight. Just stalks sticking up where the sprouts and cabbages should have been. All their hard work had been gobbled up by these tiny creatures. It was heart breaking. What led to such a phenomenon, remains a mystery to this day.

The winter progressed and soon everyone was preparing for Christmas. A flurry of excitement was everywhere. Millicent could create lovely things from very little, but she found hardly anything that she could use on the island to create anything resembling a Christmas Tree. As she had discovered when she first came to the Orkneys, it was barren and not a tree grew anywhere on it.

Upon hearing this in a letter, her father Fred took it upon himself to put that right. He bought a Christmas tree from a local shop, wrapped it up carefully and took it to the Post Office, only to be told that it was too long by 12 inches.

So, while he was there, he unpacked it and began the mammoth task of cutting off the excess. He only had his small pen-knife to do the job and it took a lot of time, blood, sweat and tears. He chipped away at the bottom of the tree with this tiny blade until at last it was done. He re-wrapped it, handed it over, paid the postage and off it went. Poor man, his hands were in a terrible state by the time he had finished.

When the tree eventually arrived at the lighthouse, word spread like wildfire and they came from all over Sanday to look at it. Some had never seen a decorated Christmas tree and it was gazed upon in wonder. Children were ushered in by their parents to behold this lovely sight. Never had families living at the lighthouse had so many visitors until the Cormacks had the Christmas Tree that year.

Lighthouse duties, however, mean that the keepers are eventually moved on to new postings and once again Dennis heard from the Northern Lighthouse Board that he had to "Pack effects ready for transfer". This time it was to the west coast of Scotland, to Corsewall Lighthouse near Stranraer. So, the family packed up their belongings and prepared to move again. They visited all the crofters before they left, to say goodbye. It was quite sad to be doing that because over the years they had all got to know each other very well and good friendships had been made. Not least, of course, were Susie and Alex Campbell at the lighthouse; it was quite a wrench to leave their friends after getting to know them so well. The couple thanked the Campbells for all their kindness and promised to keep in touch, which they duly did.

CORSEWALL LIGHTHOUSE
Stranraer

PRINCIPAL KEEPER:
Dan McGlachlan
Wife Mrs McGlachlan

Assistant Keeper:
Alistair Budge
(and mother, Mrs Budge)

Albert Christie

Mrs Olive Christie

Supernumerary:
Alec Seivewright

Supernumerary Trainee:
Wullie

Occasional Keeper:
Louis

Chapter 12

Leaving their friends, colleagues and neighbours behind them on the Orkney Islands, Millicent, Dennis and little Alistair set off on the journey to Corsewall lighthouse, near Stranraer.

Thankfully, the journey was more straightforward than the one the family had experienced from Newcastle up to the Orkneys. This time it involved the routine boat and bus journeys to the mainland, where they caught an overnight train to Glasgow Central. Thereafter it was just one more train journey to Stranraer.

The Principal Keeper at Corsewall, Dan McGlachlan, met them when they arrived in Stranraer, which was just around 11 miles from the lighthouse. Dan had business to attend to, so he told Dennis to catch a taxi there. Again, quite a difference from the trek to Start Point. It was a real luxury to load their belongings into the taxi and sit in the comfort until they reached their destination.

It was a journey of around 30 minutes. Once out of the boundaries of the town, it seemed that every field had two gates to open and close. It certainly added more time to the journey as they got in and out of the vehicle, to push and pull rusty, heavy and extremely slow-moving gates every few minutes. But they eventually got through all the fields and down the road to the lighthouse. They were shown to their flat, and once again they unpacked and prepared to make it homely and comfortable.

The very nature of the Lighthouse Service means that the accommodation buildings and tower will inevitably be in a remote area, overlooking the sea, but in comparison with Inchkeith and Orkney, it was a huge return to civilisation for the family. The town of Stranraer was close and it meant there were regular deliveries of meat and vegetables which were fresh and appetising.

Yes, Millicent was very happy with their new posting.

They all settled in at Corsewall and a new routine commenced. Millicent could travel into Stranraer and spend time shopping and when Dennis was off duty they could go in together with Alistair. Living on the mainland also meant that their family and friends could visit them and stay over.

The couple discovered that local farmers and neighbours were just as kind and generous as the people on Sanday. When they were returning to the lighthouse after a family visit, it could be the grocer or one of the farmers would get to hear of this and would pick them up from the station, take them to their own home and provide refreshments. Another driver, this time it could be the fishmonger or a different farmer, would pick them up from that house and take them in turn to their home, whereupon further refreshments would be offered. By the time they eventually reached the lighthouse Millicent said they were often stuffed to the gills with food, but these people were so incredibly kind, it proved impossible to refuse the many offers of lifts combined with food.

They had been living at Corsewall for a few months, when Dennis was seconded to cover for an absent keeper at Skerryvore lighthouse, which was further north, off the west coast of Scotland. He was taken by boat to his new posting and arrived without any undue problems. The captain of the lighthouse boat steered the vessel into what acted as a small jetty in the rocks and Dennis disembarked with his kit bag in one inelegant leap. He met his fellow keeper, Jimmy McGore, on the jetty, shook hands and they made their way over the flat rocks. The lighthouse tower was built on a small reef in the sea, and the living quarters were up in the tower. Dennis threw his kit bag over his shoulder and climbed the ladders up to the entrance, which was quite a height. This was the first time he was going to live in the actual tower of a lighthouse that was in the middle of the sea. Living in such close proximity with other keepers it was essential that everyone got on, so it was a good job he was easy going and had a good sense of humour.

His secondment to Skerryvore proved to be a dice with death as far as both Dennis and Jimmy were concerned.

It was on a particularly stormy day and the keepers were expecting a delivery of supplies from the lighthouse ship. The weather was wild and stormy, and the wind was howling, churning up the sea like a boiling mass. When they spotted the ship getting close to the jetty, Dennis and Jimmy made their way down the tower and over the rocks. The sea was crashing everywhere and the men had to take extreme care not to be swept off their feet. The captain got as close as he could into the narrow gap in the rocks and the jetty, but the swell of the sea was making it really difficult. As the men neared the ship, a great lump of sea hit them both, throwing them both into the water.

The very next wave threw Jimmy straight back onto the rocks, where he landed with a crash.

Another wave threw Dennis against the wall of the tower, whereupon his wrist got caught in a hook which was normally used to moor small boats to. The crashing waves swept him back and forwards and knocked him unconscious as he dangled there in the sea.

Jimmy rushed over as a wave receded and he managed to free Dennis from the hook and drag him to safety.

The keepers were in a sorry state. So much so that the captain of the ship reported the incident to the Northern Lighthouse office in Edinburgh. He said it had been a terrible experience for them and he felt they needed time off to recover from the shock of it all as well as their injuries.

Sadly, the company were rather unsympathetic and said the men could take holiday if they wanted. However, this was instantly declined and both men sought medical advice and took sick leave instead.

(Many years later, a documentary programme was made in respect of the lighthouse boats and steamers and the captain of that particular ship commented on something he had experienced. He went on to describe exactly what had happened to Dennis and Jimmy, being washed into the sea and then out again and added that those men were lucky to have survived such an ordeal.)

The secondment thereafter ended, Dennis recovered back at Corsewall, and life returned to normal.

Maintenance of the lighthouse buildings were always of high priority and each keeper would be assigned to particular jobs to carry out. After a discussion with Dan, the decision was made to paint the lighthouse tower. This involved someone sitting in a Bosun's Chair, which was a seat made of rope and affixed to the top of the tower and dangled to the required height while the tower surface was painted by hand. You had to have a head for heights for this job all right.

There was a light breeze when Dennis started this task but as time went on, the breeze turned into a gale and there he was, happily swinging from side to side, slapping paint on as he swung, not worried at all. However, Dan appeared below him, just as a great dollop of paint landed in front of his foot.

He looked up, saw Dennis swinging in the wind above him and shouted, "In the name of god, Dennis, get doon from there, you're making an awfy mess doon here!"

Dennis looked down at Dan and shouted back, "Aye Dan, and If I get blown down there, there'll be an even bigger mess!"

The painting stopped.

Around November 1946, Millicent had happy news for Dennis. She was once again expecting a baby, and preparations would have to be made in respect of her antenatal care and where she should have her baby.

She sought advice from her local doctor, who said that she should not stay at the lighthouse prior to the birth as it was too remote and as she had experienced a difficult birth when she had had Alistair, it was too risky. Although Stranraer wasn't too far away, the journey there involved rough terrain, fields and five farm gates to open and close. And so, it was decided that Millicent should once again return to Newcastle in advance to have her baby. There were still a few months before that would be necessary, but she discussed it all with her parents and plans were put in place.

In January 1947, Dennis was due leave and he and Millicent and Alistair travelled to St Abbs to stay with the family. It just happened that the country was experiencing one of the harshest winters on record. Snow was falling to levels never known before and when they were on the bus, they had almost reached the village but the bus got stuck in the snow within sight of the village. All the men had to get off the bus and were each given spades, and they had to dig it out again. It was a hard job and there was a lot of puffing and panting but they managed it with good humour. The bus eventually made it into the village, and it was with great relief everyone made their way to their respective homes. Not least, Dennis and pregnant Millicent and little Alistair.

When baby Pamela made her appearance in June, it was much better weather. She was born on 23rd June and was to be called Pamela Doreen, her middle name in honour of her Godmother, Nellie's good friend Doreen Sutherland. Doreen was absolutely thrilled about being given this honour, and she gave her own christening robe for Pamela to wear. This robe still remains in the family.

Dennis was still on duty at Corsewall at the time but at least he got to hear on the day of her birth that he had a daughter. They arranged the christening when Dennis had leave and all went without a hitch – apart from the baby crying her head off during the ceremony. Someone said that apparently that was lucky, but perhaps it was said in an effort to soothe everyone's ears.

Afterwards they all returned to Corsewall and Dennis returned to his duties.

A few months later, Dennis received word of his next posting, which was to be on the Isle of Man.

As was the norm, they packed up all their belongings and prepared for the move. A taxi took them to the station in Stranraer.

They travelled to the dock where the lighthouse ship would then transport them to Douglas on the Isle of Man. Once aboard, they were shown to their cabin and they put all their belongings out of the way and waited for the ship to sail. The weather, however, was not favourable and the captain would not make the decision to set sail while it persisted. Daily forecasts were sought but it was not until the fifth day that it was possible to sail. During this time, Dennis had to use the Ship to Shore phone to update the office as to the delay.

During these five days waiting for the ship to sail, Alistair had had a whale of a time. He remembered spending his fourth birthday aboard the ship and was of course full of mischief and had been scampering everywhere, aided and abetted by the crew. They had taken him under their wing and let him see the engine room, the bridge and practically anywhere he wanted to go. The result was he was absolutely scruffy and a right 'tatty bogle', as they say in those parts.

When the sun rose on the fifth day, it was beautiful and calm. The captain ordered the crew to put to sea and the ship left its moorings, much to everyone's relief.

When the ship arrived at last at the Isle of Man, the family joined everyone else up on the top deck to watch the approach into harbour. There were exclamations of surprise from other passengers when they saw baby

Pamela in her Moses basket. "Where did she come from? She must be a quiet baby, we never heard a thing!"

Everyone disembarked in Douglas and Dennis organised transport to their new home in Port St Mary. As a family, they would all be living in the lighthouse buildings there, but when he was on duty, he would be in a lighthouse tower known as the Chicken Rock, which was in the middle of the sea.

CHICKEN ROCK LIGHTHOUSE
Port St Mary
Isle of Man

PRINCIPAL KEEPER:

John Galbraith
Wife: Jessie
Son: John

Assistant Keepers:

Donald Budge

Jimmy Mainland
Wife ?
Sons: Roddy, Iain
and Norman

The Chicken Rock lighthouse was built on a small area of rock in the sea. The accommodation for the keepers is in the tower itself.

The families of all lighthouse keepers lived in the Northern Lighthouse buildings on the mainland in Port St Mary. Each family had their own flat.

Chapter 13

Dennis was given around 24 hours to get settled into their new accommodation in Port St Mary, then it was straight back to duty and over to the Chicken Rock to commence work. The lighthouse was around one and a half miles just off the Calf of Man, right in the middle of the sea. It was similar to Skerryvore with a rock base surrounding it but without the trauma of the latter. Smaller vessels could approach the area and arrivals and departures in relative safety. Keepers at that time would be on duty for two months on the Rock, and transported back to Port St Mary for one month's leave. The lighthouse boat collected him from a small jetty and ferried him and his kit bag over to the Rock.

A keeper's duties included taking temperatures, regular weather readings and recording them, and noting the sea conditions amongst other things, as well as cleaning everything brass and chrome until they shone brightly; this also included the lens of the light in the tower itself. As well as this recording and cleaning, there was maintenance of all the machinery operating the lantern. When a day's work was finished, there was still cooking and cleaning of the living quarters to do. It was not a job that gave you plenty of time to yourself just because you were miles away from civilisation – you had to cater for yourself and your fellow keepers as well. But of course, you did have days off, when the other keepers would be carrying out the required duties. Those days were yours, when you could catch up on letter writing or reading, or doing whatever hobbies you were interested in. Dennis was a dab hand at making things to fill in his leisure times. He carved wooden items, such as a yacht and a wheelbarrow, for example, and even put his hand to making rugs with small pieces of material (sometimes referred to as 'clippy mats'). Spare time was never wasted in the lighthouse service.

Millicent liked living in Port St Mary very much. The accommodation was one of four independent flats, each being occupied by keepers and their families, and theirs was on the ground floor. Best of all, she had both hot and cold taps! What a welcome luxury that was. There were other houses nearby in this little town, as well as shops and a school, all within walking distance. Over the road and down a few steps was a lovely cove and sandy beach.

Alistair started at the nearby school, and when Millicent had dropped him off there, she would enjoy the lovely walk back. She had Pamela in her pram and it was a good way to get to know the neighbours as she made her way home. There is nothing like a baby in a pram to start a conversation in a small community, and very soon, Millicent got to know a lot of her neighbours without any trouble at all.

While Dennis was away on duty, however, she became increasingly worried about the fact that as soon as any man looked in the pram, the minute she clapped eyes on him, Pamela would scream her head off. Women were fine, and it wasn't any particular man she objected to, it was all of them. Millicent fretted away, thinking that when he came home on leave and got the same response, Dennis would be devastated. As it turned out, she needn't have worried. During his time away, he had grown a beard, and when he lifted the child up in his arms to speak to her, she was fascinated and just looked at him in wonder. No tears were shed, much to Millicent's relief.

Family life at the lighthouse buildings was sometimes very trying, as Millicent was to discover. The Cormack family lived in one of the four flats, and the others were occupied by other keepers' families, each with different levels of consideration for others. There came a particular spell whereby the outside gate kept being left open, which was of great interest to Alistair when out on his daily bike rides. It was exciting for him to escape the relevant safety of the lighthouse boundaries but too hair-raising for his mother. After once more discovering her son happily peddling along the main road and her dragging him home again, the riot act was loudly made to all and sundry. Dire consequences would follow if everyone did not heed her demand that the gate MUST be kept shut at all times. No-one messes with a mother when she is protecting her young. Things settled down once more and the gate was duly kept closed more diligently.

Occasionally her strength of character was called upon when having to stand up to officials at the Office. They once informed her that a short-stay keeper needed accommodation when he was coming to attend to repairs and maintain the buildings, and considering Dennis was on duty at the Rock, she should be able to offer spare room. They were politely but firmly informed that she was a married woman and if her husband was not at home on leave, she would absolutely not have another man staying overnight in her home. When and only when her husband was on shore leave, she would happily oblige. She had no objections then. The Office eventually learned to accept that she meant what she said, and no amount of persuading could get her to change her mind, and they would have to organise alternative accommodation for the visitors.

When Dennis was on his month's leave, they would have a break away and visit families at Newcastle or St Abbs. One such visit to St Abbs proved particularly memorable. When word spread that the family had arrived, friends of Dennis called in at Ocean View to greet them all. They made a great fuss of Pamela, who was not quite walking yet and hence was putty in their hands. She was also susceptible to all kinds of mischief by these so-called friends. They got themselves into the kitchen while Dennis was cooking kippers and scoured the cupboard for other delicacies. They concocted a disgusting variety of culinary delights including custard, jam, cake and of course the said kippers. To the delight of some and horror of others, she ate the lot with gusto. Millicent said in later years that she blamed those men absolutely for making her daughter so fussy about everything she ate thereafter. She would look at whatever was put in front of her, sniff it, and if she didn't like the look or the smell, would flatly refuse to eat it.

The Isle of Man was a very accessible for visitors and Millicent was always happy when her parents were able to visit. They would sometimes come when Dennis was on duty, which broke up the months of Millicent being alone with the two children. There were lovely walks to go on and they all became a regular sight walking around Port St Mary with Pamela in her pram. When Alistair was off school, they sometimes caught the bus into the capital, Douglas.

There were no televisions around at this time and radio was king. The island turned out to be a popular venue for celebrities of both the radio and film world wanting a quiet holiday. Millicent and her parents were out on one of their morning walks when they spotted Wilfred Pickles. He had a very popular radio show and was well known for the phrase "What's on the table, Mabel?" – Mabel was his wife and fellow presenter of the show. Millicent had her camera in her bag for an opportunity such as this and quickly whipped it out and took a photo as Wilfred passed by. She did wonder if Mabel was on the island too.

Another popular radio show was called 'Down Your Way' and one of the stars was Frankie Ingleman. So, when he was spotted, another furore developed amongst loyal fans who were thrilled to discover another star was amongst them.

An even bigger star, however, was Jack Warner from the world of film. It was early in his career, but he was credited with some well received films by the time he was seen on the island. He later appeared in the film The Blue Lamp in 1950 when he played a London bobby called George Dixon. That film was so successful that a series called Dixon of Dock Green was created for television in which he starred as the main character – despite the fact that he had been killed off in the film. Families would settle down on a Saturday night to be entertained by gritty crime stories which always ended well, with George saying a few wise words under the Police lamp.

Millicent managed to get an autographed photo of Jack, which she treasured and kept amongst her memorabilia of photos.

Millicent's sister-in-law Elsie also came over for a short stay and brought young Dennis with her. As usual, the prefix 'young' was always attached to his name and this continued well into adulthood. It was nice for Alistair to spend time with his cousin as they were of similar age and as the beach was just over the road, they all spent a lot of time relaxing in the summer sun on the sands. The cove was a quiet and gentle area for families to spend time together and relax, being especially popular at weekends.

Millicent would also travel back to Newcastle with the children when Dennis was on his two-month duty. Because she would spend a few weeks there, she enrolled Alistair in school there to continue with his education. When returning home to the Isle of Man, he would once again attend his local school. It must have been quite difficult for a young child to have to adjust to being taught at two different schools by different people, not to mention the added problem of trying to form friendships with other pupils. But somehow, Alistair rose to the challenge on both counts and made good progress.

Millicent was always busy and even found fun ways to include the children in household chores. Pamela was growing into a very independent little girl, full of energy. So, to run off this energy, Millicent would tie dusters to her feet and those of Alistair too, and they would skate around and polish the floor. It was great fun.

Back on leave, Dennis's passion for football had never waned and as soon as he was back from the Rock, members of the local team would be straight round to book him for the very next game, and of course he was more than happy to oblige.

If Fred and Nellie were visiting, the whole family would accompany Dennis to the match too. Nellie said after the first half of a particular match "Eh, what a dirty player Dennis is". Of course, he wasn't, just enthusiastic. He wasn't very tall but his little legs could go like the clappers when he was running for the ball.

During one game, he was very disgruntled to be sent off after an altercation with an opposing player. When the game ended, he was spotted digging a hole by the side line and the referee walked up to him and asked what he was doing. Dennis looked up and said with a twinkle in his eye, "It's for you, for sending me off!" It was all in good humour of course, both given and taken, thankfully.

When he was on duty back on the Chicken Rock, one of the jobs that needed doing was the painting of the lighthouse and Dennis was up on the dome of the lighthouse, diligently working away with his painting task. Further south of the lighthouse on the mainland was an RAF base and when the pilots were on exercises or testing their planes, they flew up the coastline and banked around a particular landmark and returned to base. The particular landmark was the lighthouse. So, when Dennis spotted the plane overhead, he gave them a friendly wave. Perhaps the pilot believed the keeper was in difficulty or had a problem, but he banked his aircraft and flew back over the tower. Poor Dennis was almost blown off the dome with the backdraft and clung on for dear life. He never waved again after that.

One of the nearest shops to the flat was the local ice cream shop who served up the most delicious home-made ices. Millicent had recently consulted her new doctor on the island because young Pamela would not drink milk no matter how she tried to disguise it. She was around three years old at the time and Millicent was most concerned that the lack of calcium in her youngster's diet put her at risk of things such as rickets and brittle bones.

The doctor took her to the ice cream parlour where after a chat with the proprietor, they were taken into their preparation rooms so that Millicent could see exactly what went into making the ice cream. The proprietor and doctor explained all the goodness in the ingredients were more than enough to alleviate her concerns. Before they left, Millicent was told to let little Pamela call in any time and he would give her the ice-cream of her choice, and he would be happy to get payment the next time the family called in. This arrangement proved a huge success. Pamela did indeed toddle off to the shop on her own, with Mother looking on of course, and in minutes, she would reappear out of the shop, happily tucking into her treat and making her way home.

Millicent and the children continued to live in Port St Mary while Dennis worked on the Chicken Rock, but unforeseen circumstances were soon to change all that. In 1950, Millicent's father Fred suddenly died and everyone's future took a very different direction.

Chapter 14

Millicent's father, Fred Oliver, sadly passed away very unexpectedly. Nellie was devastated at the death of her husband and made it clear that she felt unable to live on her own, despite being quite a young woman. Initially, Fred junior and his wife Elsie came to live with Nellie to support her and help her adjust to life without her husband. Unfortunately, it became increasingly obvious that this could not be a permanent arrangement as the women did not get on. It is not an easy scenario, sharing a home with your mother-in-law, and for Elsie, it was no exception.

The whole family met together to talk things through and try to come up with a solution to the problem. Millicent's strong family values were brought to a head and following discussions privately with Dennis, it was decided that they would have to leave the lighthouse service and come to live in Newcastle to support her mother. It meant a huge change in circumstances for everyone and a quite sad end to the hopes and dreams of their future family life in the Northern Lighthouse Service.

This was further proof of the unquestionable love that the couple had for each other. In the first instance, Millicent had sacrificed the career she had loved and a good way of life to marry the man she loved and had taken on all the hardships that his job meant for her. And now, Dennis was preparing to leave the job he loved to live in a city with his mother-in-law and leave the outdoor life he had always known.

Dennis handed in his notice to the Head Office in Edinburgh and at the end of his duty, they left Port St Mary on the Isle of Man and moved to Eaglescliffe Drive, Cochrane Park in Newcastle upon Tyne.

Dennis managed to get a job working for the Ministry in Longbenton, and soon after, Millicent returned to nursing, joining the staff at the Sanderson Hospital in Gosforth.

The Sanderson Hospital had originally been a children's hospital until around 1948 but when the NHS was introduced in 1947, adult patients were thereafter also treated there, some of whom were long-stay patients.

Millicent soon adjusted to being back in her nursing role and threw herself into the hard work of caring for the sick and injured. She became well-known for her no-nonsense approach to her work, and one task in particular: the removal of sticky dressings. Men especially dreaded the removal of these dressings from their hairy legs. Most of the nurses pulled the dressings a little at a time until they were completely off, which just prolonged the agony. Millicent, however, would take hold of one edge and just rip it off in one go! They came to realise that Millicent's way was excruciatingly painful but over in a trice. So, Millicent was somewhat reluctantly requested for such procedures. Their pain was inevitable, but thankfully over very quickly.

Her children, however, weren't of the same opinion. Pamela in particular did want a plaster to be removed quickly but hated what she knew was to come, and would whimper in the lead up to it, saying "Ohhh Mam! No! It's gonna hurt..." but by the time she had finished the sentence, it was off. That memory is still strongly remembered!

Millicent worked at the Sanderson for a good few years and made some special friends there. Nurse Louise Kay was her best friend, however. She was a tiny bundle of energy, but an excellent nurse, especially in an operating theatre where she exceeded in assisting the surgeons. She often had Millicent in stitches when they had to hurry along a hospital corridor when Louise would skip up the wall, kick her heels and land back down again without missing a step. When Louise met her future husband Alan,

Millicent and Dennis attended the wedding, and later when their sons Antony and Christopher were born, they were godparents. Dennis and Alan, in much later years, both joined the Freemasons and remained good friends too.

Alistair started school at Cragside Junior School in Heaton, and later, Pamela joined him at the same school, albeit in the Infants section. They both learned that birthdays there were very exciting because you were given a Smartie for each year of your birth. Unfortunately for Pamela, she sometimes missed out on this treat because her birthday fell during an annual week's holiday known locally as Race Week. Sometimes the teachers would remember and give her the treat upon return to school, but other times, Pamela would have to remind them!

Race Week was a North East annual holiday for local mineworkers, which culminated in a horse race at Gosforth Racecourse historically known as the 'Pitman's Derby' and continues to this day. One year, Millicent's Uncle Norman had at the time purchased a beautiful horse from Ireland and much to the delight of the family, his horse won the main event!

Race week was also known for it being the week a huge fair took place on the Newcastle Town Moor. It was the largest gathering of funfair travellers and they would come from all over the country to meet up with friends and family every year.

And so, the family settled into a new routine and learned how to live with Nellie. Having young children around could sometimes prove difficult for her but she would have to learn too that the alternative of living on her own would not be to her liking either. Millicent, of course, knew her mother and her ways, but it was a new experience for Dennis. His happy-go-lucky nature made the transition from his past way of life to this present one a lot easier than it might have been.

His sense of humour could often save the day if both women were unhappy about anything, a funny quip or daft face would result in raising a laugh between them. A lesser man might not have been able to handle difficult situations as well as he.

Nellie's good friend Doreen Sutherland still lived across the road and was the only person nearby who owned a telephone. One day she came hurrying across and urgently rang the bell, telling them there was a call for Dennis from his father. It was worrying news. His Aunt Jeannie was ill and the menfolk at Ocean View were struggling to care for her. She had always been the one looking after them and did absolutely everything for them. What was to be done? Could anyone there help?

Deep conversations followed and it seemed obvious that Millicent, being a nurse, should be the one who was in the best position to offer the help that was so desperately needed. They discussed how they could make things work if she was to go to St Abbs to nurse Jeannie. If Nellie was able to make sure the children got to school and came home to a cooked meal at the end of the day, Dennis could muck in with the washing and cooking when he was not at work. His experience of self-sufficiency in the lighthouse service certainly paid dividends at this time. 'Granny Nellie' as he called her, said she was certainly happy to do this.

Poor Jeannie was in a sorry state when Millicent eventually arrived at Ocean View. She was lying in the bed set in the wall in the small main room in the 'side house', possibly because it was the warmest place, having the fire lit in the range there. She lay on coarse blankets, with more coarse blankets on top, old pillows and a nighty that had seen better days too. Millicent lost no time in correcting all this. She gently got her out of bed and settled her in a chair next to the fire and wrapped her up in the blankets. She stripped the bed right down to the mattress, then raided the linen cupboard of all the best sheets and blankets inside. It made no sense to keep things for 'best' when they were never used for what they were made for. She put fresh clean sheets on the mattress, top and bottom, fresh cotton pillowcases and soft blankets. There were new nighties too for Jeannie to wear. It must have been at least a small comfort to Jeannie when at last she was back in bed, in soft clean bedding.

Nellie and Dennis shared their time to look after Alistair and Pamela and ensured their day-to-day routine continued as normal. Dennis wrote regularly to Millicent, telling her what they had been up to and reassured her that all was well at home. He wrote his heartfelt thanks to her in those letters for all she was doing for Jeannie. She had played such a big part in his and his brother Jim's upbringing during their childhood and she was very special to them.

The days turned into weeks and Millicent diligently continue to care for Jeannie until she was well again. As soon as she thought Jeannie was fit enough to be left in the care of her brothers, Millicent prepared to return home. With the worry of the last few weeks and the knowledge that without her help, they would have really struggled, the men's gratitude was evident. Stronger family bonds had been created and it was great affection they saw her off at the train station for her journey back to Newcastle.

Life returned to normal and everyone resumed their previous roles.

Dennis left his job in the Ministry at Longbenton and started work at George Angus, a factory which made oil seals, initially in Walker but then moved to a new large factory built next to the Coast Road. As the family home was a five-minute walk to the Coast Road, transport to work was much better. It was a very well-paid job, which meant that the family were able to save up and eventually, after a few years, purchase their very first car. It was a maroon coloured Hillman Minx (ABR 670); and a few years later, a blue and cream Ford Consul (NYX 568).

Millicent soldiered on with nursing but was gradually tiring of her shift-work at the Sanderson. It often involved working unsociable hours, and travelling to and from the hospital on two or three buses could prove challenging and sometimes impossible in bad weather. It didn't help that public transport was often unreliable, which sometimes made her late for duty.

It was after such an event that she saw advertised and applied for a job at a day nursery in the West End of Newcastle. It would mean daytime hours only, weekends off, and only one bus journey. She was thrilled to be asked to attend for an interview, and even more thrilled when she was offered the job. Not only would it make her working life so much easier, it meant that once again she would be doing what she loved best: working with babies and young children.

It was also a move that meant an indirect involvement in one of the most infamous and notorious child murders in the country.

Memories

"I remember Gran meeting me off the school bus on my first day at Cragside Infants' School."

Pamela and Millicent were sitting chatting as usual on a Sunday afternoon.

"And she asked me how I had liked school."

"I was at work at the hospital when you started school," said Millicent, "but your Gran would tell me all about the things you got up to when I got home."

"My only comments were that school was OK but I didn't like the noise everyone else made on the bus. They were far too loud!"

"I had forgotten that."

"And speaking of bus journeys, you remember when we would all catch the bus over to Washington to visit Uncle Fred and Aunt Elsie?"

"Of course, I do. We had to catch two buses there, and two buses back; it took ages. But in those days, that was how you kept in touch with your family, you visited each other. They didn't have a telephone and neither did we."

"I remember listening to the engine on the Washington bus for some reason, and what I now know to be the change through the gears; at that time I thought the engine breathed like humans. I would hum to myself at exactly the same time, taking a breath at each gear change. This was fine until it reached the top gear. I could never figure out how it could manage to keep going for such a long time without taking another breath. I couldn't do it, no matter how hard I tried. It was always a puzzle!"

"Eh, the funny things children think," said Millicent.

"I remember as well when you and Dad set me up after I asked if my new best friend Sylvia from school could come for tea. This was a big thing for me, I had never asked a friend to come for tea before. It was going to be on a Friday, and you always had kippers on a Friday. Dad had my leg pulled well and truly. I didn't like the smell of kippers so would never eat them. Dad said if I tried them, I could have some 'kipper-dip' afterwards. He said it was a lovely drink made from the juices of the kippers and was a real treat. But I was having none of it."

Millicent laughed, remembering it well. "Your dad loved to pull your leg, he was a divvil at times."

"He told me to check with Sylvia that she liked kippers, just in case that was what we had. If she had a kipper, she could have the kipper-dip. I was so embarrassed having to ask her, but I did, and she said she was sure it would be ok. I remember on the day, though, there was a lovely spread on the table. Sandwiches, scones and cakes. Not a sign of a kipper anywhere. It was after that I discovered exactly what 'kipper-dip' was. Just washing up water that was put in the pan and left until after tea. It was never a delicious drink, it had just been a ruse to encourage me to try the fish. I still never ate any kippers!"

Chapter 15

Woodland Crescent Day Nursery was established in an old farmhouse in one of the poorest areas of the city, run by the council to support parents with a desire to work, or who needed help in caring for their children. The aim was to enhance the lives of babies and toddlers, both mentally and physically, and to advise parents on their welfare when required. While they were at the nursery, they would be well fed and stimulated on a daily basis and time was taken to prepare them for entry into school when they reached the appropriate age.

Working there was both challenging and fulfilling and Millicent settled into her new role with great enthusiasm. Her days of purgatory during enforced piano lessons when she was young were soon forgotten when she played nursery rhymes for the children and she saw how much they loved to sing and dance. Millicent was also a talented artist and she painted friezes for the nursery walls, depicting nursery rhyme characters and Disney scenes. The children loved those too.

As the years passed, Millicent was promoted to Matron and she took over responsibility for the nursery together with managing both nursing and support staff. She was very strict, as always, but also good fun.

Whenever a parent arrived late to collect their chid, they would be reminded of the appropriate time they should have been there. After all, she too had a bus to catch home. All this as well as dealing with particularly difficult and sometimes abusive parents. Her authority was nevertheless always accepted and respected.

The role of Matron also involved meetings at the Civic Centre with Matrons from other nurseries in Newcastle, as well as council members. Woodland Crescent was also a centre for Health Visitors and they had an office within the building. Their duties were mainly visiting new mothers to check both their health and that of their baby. Millicent was always on hand to discuss cases and offer advice when needed.

Millicent ensured that the children got to celebrate special times of the year, such as Easter and Christmas. A police sergeant from the West End Police station came every year to act as Father Christmas and he was built for the part. He loved that job, and the children in turn loved him back. Each child received a present and would go home happy.

One particular little boy must have touched Millicent's heart because after a chat with his mother, she and Dennis took him away from Scotswood and into the countryside. The joy on his face during these outings was so evident, especially when he was also taken to the seaside. It had been many years before that the couple had been able to buy a car of their own, and it had opened up so many opportunities for the family and their wider circle, not least of all, these sorts of outings.

Life was a lot easier these days; the children were getting older and more independent. Nellie had an organised social week for herself – the pictures with her friend Doreen Sutherland who lived over the road, and a weekly visit to the Over 60s club – and she was happy with her family around her. Dennis's happy and mischievous nature ensured a happy mother-in-law and they got on very well. She couldn't help but laugh at him when he brought the washing in when it was really cold, and he would hold up her large knickers saying, "Eh look at your drawers, Granny Nellie, they're frozen stiff".

Their life was very different to that in the lighthouse service and possibly not so eventful, but it was by no means boring or mundane. There were always events throughout the year that brought a different kind of happiness, closer family relationships, continued meetings with friends, outings in the countryside or to the coast, and holidays to mention but a few.

Dennis and Millicent had new friends and neighbours around them, and of course having a car meant trips out in the country at weekends, and Dennis could resume his love of river fishing. When he had lived at St Abbs, he had been good friends with a man who lived in Coldingham, Forsythe Lindores, who had painstakingly taught him the art of fly fishing. Sy, as he was known, was a real character and well known in the area, with a plethora of stories and experience. (Pamela and Alistair thought for many years that his name was actually Siren Dors because that's what it sounded like when spoken.)

Often Millicent would go with Dennis when he went fishing and she would draw riverside scenes in her sketchbook. Later when at home, she would paint the scenes. It was nice for both of them to be out in the fresh air and enjoy the countryside. She had also joined a pottery painting class, and together with her daughter, they created some lovely dishes and wall plates. Her pièce de résistance was a beautiful china tea set and teapot decorated in her hand painted sweet pea design.

Working at George Angus, Dennis had joined their Sports & Social club. He had learned that they had a football team and, once again, Dennis involved himself in playing for the team. They usually played on a Saturday morning and the family would pile in the car and go to watch him battle it out on the pitch. Millicent, Nellie and the children would shout encouragement from the side-lines, while his work mates would be shouting all sorts of insults. "Come on, Dennis, wake up and get a move on, you're not at work now, you know". He was still a very skilful player albeit a little bit slower these days, but his little legs would still go like the clappers when needed. He wasn't averse to fouling opposing players either, and Nellie was not impressed when this happened. She was known to comment on the way home, as she had done when they were on the Isle of Man, "Eh, Dennis Cormack, what a dirty player you are!" but he just laughed.

Then there was the annual event of the Sports Day. And the annual Tug of War between the George Angus Team and the Scottish and Newcastle Brewery Men. Never was the tale of David and Goliath such an apt comparison between these two teams. The Brewery men were like Titans, and the Angus men were absolutely no match for them. But what they lacked in physical muscle, their determination and spirit certainly made up for it. On the one side would be these huge giants of men, physically powerful with shifting large barrels of beer every day, and on the other side were a team of mix-match males, of various heights, weight, shape and declining fitness. And right on the end was the anchor-man, Dennis. He hacked away at the ground to make a good foothold, with the hope that it would prevent him and his team from being thrust forward at the first pull. It wouldn't have mattered how deep he dug the hole; it wouldn't have made any difference. Hearts like lions the lot of them, they still got beat every year. But you never know, maybe next time…

Summer holidays were always spent in Scotland. Millicent would book a caravan for the first week and off they would go with Alistair, Pamela and cousin Dennis too. Whenever they could, they would visit different lighthouses to visit former colleagues and friends. The second week was spent at St Abbs. Ocean View was always made available for the family to stay. It was a huge house with lots of bedrooms, as well as the living areas in the annexe, so there was always plenty of room.

Over time, Peter, Danny and Jeannie had all passed away, which resulted in Tommy living on his own. He was not in the best of health and after family discussions, Jim and Eileen decided they would move their family from where they were living in Edinburgh and go back to St Abbs. Jim was currently working on the Norwegian whaling boats and could be away at sea for months at a time and it was a hard job. One such trip cost him his forefinger when an accident sheered it straight off. It seemed a good time for change. Jim would make a living as the Cormacks had always done, by making creels to catch lobsters and crabs. Eileen would run the family home and would care for Tommy as well. She later found work in the local grocery shop in the village, just along the road.

Jim had left the lighthouse service because when he learned that his next posting was to be on Eilean Mor, one of the Flannan Islands, he refused to go and resigned from the company. A great mystery surrounded the Flannan Isle and still does to this day.

It was in 1900, after a spell of bad weather, that a relief lighthouse keeper had been transported over to the island aboard the Hesperus, but when he and the crew arrived on the island, it was evident that something was not right. There was no-one on the landing dock to meet them, and when the group travelled up to the lighthouse and went inside, there was no sign at all of the three keepers who should be there. The table was set, food on the plates, and a chair overturned on the floor. A search of the area revealed nothing. The men fired a rocket in case the keepers were somewhere out of sight and sound of their calls but there was no response. The island inherited an air of superstition and notoriety. What had happened to the men? Why was there no trace at all to be found of them? Investigations seemed to raise more questions than answers.

Irrational as it may be, many people are superstitious and living in this small village of St Abbs, fishing families particularly so. And the Cormacks were definitely in that bracket, which must have been a large part of Jim's decision not to go to Eilean Mor.

For instance, if they were on their way down to the harbour to go out to sea and it looked as if they were going to have to pass a woman, they would turn around and go back home, because this was considered extremely unlucky. Strange but true.

Holidays there meant that the two families got to spend time together again, which was lovely, and always fun. The cousins spent a lot of time together and good friendships flourished. Nellie would come too and, occasionally, sisters Lucy and Eppie, as well as Doreen Sutherland.

Nellie always had her own summer holidays away and would either go somewhere new with Doreen Sutherland, or visit family in various parts of the country. Millicent and Dennis continued to head north to Scotland.

At the end of these holidays, when everyone was back at home, it was a case of trying to get a word in edgeways because everyone wanted to talk about what they did while they were away.

Easter was spent at St Abbs over a few days and traditions were not only 'rolling' your egg at Starney, you also 'dunched' your hardboiled egg by having a bashing competition with an opponent. That never lasted long either, they always eventually cracked and disintegrated! Millicent brought any leftover hot cross buns which the cook had made at the nursery and were surplus to requirements. These were eaten with relish by all.

St Abbs was a wonderful place, with the most marvellous area names, such as Pettico Wick, the little rocky bay called Starney and even a hill called the Homeli Knowe which overlooked the beach at Coldingham sands. The place of Dennis' birth became very special to all of his family and was loved by them all.

Other holidays throughout the year would always be spent at St Abbs too. Most of the time was spent either down at the harbour or out in the Beaver, fishing or swimming around it.

One incident happened during one of these trips and was often referred to when comparing 'funny stories'. Out at sea in the Beaver with the family one day, Dennis was taking a fish off the hook, and was studiously concentrating on the manoeuvre when all of a sudden, he dropped the fish and started shouting and gesticulating frantically, rattling his ear with his hand. Because some fish had already been caught, cleaned and their innards thrown out of the boat, the seagulls were flying all around awaiting the next lot. And one had done a huge poo, which had landed right in his ear. What a shot! As Dennis put it, "The whole of the North Sea yet that bloody bird had to get me right in the ear!" It was very funny.

One day, their old friend Will Wilson and his wife were in Newcastle and were invited for tea. They were all sitting round the table enjoying fish and chips, and Dennis was regaling a particularly good story about 'the one that got away' during a recent fishing trip on the river Coquet. He was in full swing, demonstrating with his arms how he had cast his line when, bang! He sent the nearby budgie cage flying – all over the table. As well as the cage, the bird was flapping around inside so that feathers, seed, water and grit scattered everywhere and, of course, all over the fish and chips. It was quite some time before they managed to stop laughing. Eventually the bird and the cage were reinstated, and the seeded contents of their tea was thrown out. Dennis once again was sent off to the chip shop to purchase more food, seeing as the disaster had all been his fault.

When another friend from St Abbs, David Aitchison, was working aboard a whaling ship, it came into the Quayside in Newcastle, so the family drove down there to see him. It was a huge, impressive vessel and contained below deck a complete factory where whale meat was processed, and oil extracted. Dennis and Alistair were keen to go down below to see where all this happened, and so was Pamela. However, she got as far as the door leading down below deck and couldn't bear the smell, so she stayed up top with her mother. She was intrigued to see at sundown, a crew member drew down the flag from the flagpole, while whistling the 'Last Post' as he did it. With the setting sun shining through the arches of the Tyne Bridge it was a very atmospheric and peaceful scene there on the Tyne, despite being aboard a vessel which in later years was considered to be very controversial.

Every New Year's Eve, the event was celebrated on television with a show from Scotland. It was called the White Heather Club, starring Jimmy Shand who was famous for playing the accordion, and singers Kenneth McKellar and Andy Stewart, amongst others. The programme was very popular and was of course always watched by the family. It was a little bit of Scotland in the home in Newcastle. On one particular show, an actor called Duncan MacRae appeared. He was known for playing the part of Para Handy, who was the skipper of a Clyde puffer called the Vital Spark and who got up to all sorts of mischief in his endeavour to make money and avoid authority and their regulations. It was a brilliantly funny show and never missed by the Cormacks. He was not known for singing at all, but on this night, he sang a song called 'A Wee Cock Sparra" and Dennis sat watching it, in fits of laughter. The song got funnier as it went on, and Dennis laughed all the harder. Needless to say, everyone else caught on as well and joined in. It was a revelation. It was the funniest thing to have ever appeared on the show in their opinion. Every year after that, they all would wait in anticipation to hear if Duncan was going to appear again, and of course he did, and once again he would sing the same song by popular demand, much to the joy of the family.

Also in demand on New Year's Eve (or Auld Year's Night as it was also known), was Dennis. He was jolly, good fun, could sing and play the accordion and of course he was Scottish. And as we all know: the Scots know how to party especially on this night. As Dennis would say, he could play anything as long as it was Scottish. His beloved, tatty accordion would once again be brought out of the bottom of the wardrobe, stuck together with more sticky tape – which hopefully would keep it all together – and off the family would go in a procession to visit the neighbours who were eagerly awaiting their arrival. Doors were always open to 'First Foots' and Dennis inevitably was first to hopefully bring good luck to each family they visited. As soon as he entered the house, he would be offered a glass of golden whisky, which he always took with appreciation, but secretly and despite the belief that Scots and whisky go together, he did not really like the stuff. But on this night, he never refused the kindness shown by others, and would break into song, as expected and hoped, 'Auld Lang Syne' and 'Come Home Paddy Reilly', to name just two of his repertoire.

It was the one night in the year that he ended up 'steaming' and rather worse for wear. The amount of whisky that was thrust upon him, it was hardly surprising. It was also the only night he knew Millicent would not give him a flea in his ear for such behaviour as well.

Each year, more doors would open and neighbours became friends because of the celebrations held on that night.

In 1966 there was a big family celebration when Alistair and his fiancée Edith got married. Each sibling was a bridesmaid – Irene and Pamela; cousin Dennis was best man and his brother Alan was an usher. Alistair was now working at Newcastle Airport and was doing well helping run the Export Department at BKS. In 1970 BKS changed its name to Northeast Airlines. Alistair and Edith had a daughter Susan in 1971 and a son Iain in 1975. In 1976 Northeast Airlines integrated into British Airways. When the department was later closed and the staff made redundant, Alistair and two colleagues decided to create their own company. They won the contract with British Airways. It proved to be an excellent decision and the company was very successful.

On 25th July 1967, Millicent and Dennis celebrated their Silver Wedding and they had a great big party where as many of their friends and family who could come, joined in the fun. There was lots of music and dancing, of course, but the main event was when once again, Dennis, his brother Jim, and friend Will Wilson stood on the stage together and sang like they had done 25 years earlier, "Be Nobody's Darling but Mine" to Millicent. For those who had attended their wedding, it was like travelling back in time to that lovely day. The three men were still in fine voice and it was a truly moving gesture.

When they finished, everyone applauded, and they were rewarded with a nice cold beer.

The following year, Pamela married Ken and they in turn had Karen and Craig to complete their little family.

Memories

"Do you remember when we were on holiday at St Abbs one year when the lifeboat was called out?"

"I do! It was in the middle of the night, wasn't it?"

"I got such a shock! The rockets had gone up, in a huge bang, and all the men could be seen running down to the harbour. I stood by the bedroom window and watched them."

"Your Dad went down too, but he wasn't as quick by then and they had a full crew by the time he got there."

Tommy was a lot older these days and not working on the lifeboat but nevertheless, when the rockets went up, his natural instinct kicked in and he found himself dressed and outside with all the others in minutes.

You could see the lights going on in the houses all around the village. When the lifeboat was called out, everyone was alerted in a communal spirit.

"Then Dad came back and told us what was happening. A yacht had got into difficulties just off St Abbs Head and was drifting towards the rocks – hence the emergency and the callout."

"Eh, then we all piled in the car and went to Eyemouth to see them coming in."

When the family had arrived at the harbour, the lifeboat and yacht were safely moored up. Dennis called out to the lifeboat crew and chatted to the men. They had all been invited to have a 'wee dram' aboard the yacht as a small token of thanks.

"Your dad declined his invitation to join them, but not before he noticed his pal David Aitchison was minus his beautiful smile – his teeth being still at home in a jar of water, and another crew member having his pyjamas peeping through his waterproofs and hair like he'd been dragged through a hedge backwards."

There was never a minute to spare when the lifeboat was needed. It never mattered what condition you were in when you got to the lifeboat station, it was just vital that you got there the quickest you possibly could.

"And then it was back in the car, back to St Abbs, and back to bed!"

Chapter 16

The nursery being in a poor area of Newcastle, unfortunately rendered it at risk of being broken into now and again and, inevitably, the police would call at Eaglescliffe Drive to ask Millicent to attend as she was the key holder. Dennis would take her in the car and they would go into the building together to see what damage had been done.

In 1968 they were asked again by the police to attend and what the couple found was complete devastation. All the containers in the kitchen which held dry ingredients, flour, sugar etc., had been emptied all over the floor. There was mess everywhere. Additionally, there was writing on the wall, referring to Martin Brown, a four-year-old little boy who had been found dead in May of that year, together with handwritten little notes admitting responsibility for his death.

The police investigating this break-in subsequently discovered it was two young local girls who had vandalised the nursery and the matter went to court. Millicent had to attend the court as a witness and saw first-hand the relationship between one mother and child, and it wasn't good. Alongside the youngest girl was her slightly older friend. It was evident to Millicent that the girls were not fazed at all about being in the court as they laughed and giggled to each other until the Judge eventually asked the parents to speak to their children and remind them of the seriousness of where they were and why.

The girls were Mary Bell and her friend Norma Bell (no relation).

There was no proof the girls were involved in the murder of Martin Brown, despite the written notes – it seemed too far-fetched that such young girls could be responsible for such a thing.

Two months after the break-in, another little boy was found murdered. He was three-year-old Brian Howe, who was a regular at the nursery and who Millicent knew very well. She had missed him when he had not turned up as usual. He had always called her "Cormack", never Matron, and would always pull at her clothes when he wanted her attention. She was devastated to learn from the police what had happened to him. She made an office available to them to be used as a control centre while enquiries were ongoing.

As it was, and as has been widely covered in all medias, it was revealed that indeed, Mary and Norma had been involved in both boys' murders. Norma, despite being the older child, was found to be totally under the influence of the younger Mary and was acquitted. Mary was found guilty of manslaughter on the grounds of diminished responsibility. Her family background was revealed as problematic and had a great deal to do with how she had developed.

The case was something which affected Millicent deeply, especially as she personally knew one of the boys and the whole thing was brought closer to home because of that and the fact that the police presence in the nursery for weeks on end meant there was no respite from it.

The support she received from her husband and family was exactly what she needed and helped her through this most difficult time of her life.

Chapter 17

In the Spring of 1969, suddenly and unexpectedly, Millicent's mother Nellie died. After the funeral, the couple were suddenly living on their own, the first time since they married in 1942. It would be a strange experience, planning things for just the two of them instead of including her mother into the equation. Their friends Raymond and Betty Pike were a tremendous support to the couple immediately and it was Raymond who visited Pamela and Ken living in Sandyford to break the sad news.

When their first grandchild Karen arrived later that month, once again, a happy glow was experienced at Eaglescliffe Drive. Dennis would collect Millicent from the nursery as usual and then call in at Sandyford to see the baby. Millicent would help with little jobs that needed doing during the first few weeks after the baby arrived. As Karen grew older, she would stay overnight with them and once again the family Moses basket came into use. Christmas that year was especially special with a new baby in the family gathering.

When Dennis was encouraged to join the Freemasons by close friends in that organisation, it opened up all manner of social events. There were many dinner dances to go to and Millicent thoroughly enjoyed meeting up with their friends at almost all of them. She loved putting on all her refinery and accumulated some very stunning evening dresses as a result. One of these evenings, however, was in fancy dress. Dennis attended as a hula hula girl, complete with Hawaiian garland and grass skirt. When he rustled off to the toilets to answer a call of nature, unfortunately he got his grass skirt stuck in his zip. His friend Clem Clark came into the gents as Dennis was attempting to free the said grass, so he kneeled down in front of him to see if he could do better. Just at that moment, a stranger came into the room, took one look at the scene (picture it if you will), and said "Oops, sorry!" turned heel and went straight back out again! The wives could not understand why the two men came back later in hysterics. It was quite some time before they calmed down enough to be able to tell them.

There was a very exciting event in the family the following year in 1970 when Dennis caught the first salmon of the season on the River Coquet. This was an annual event which he had taken part in for years, but this year he did indeed land the very first salmon. It was a great achievement after years of trying.

By tradition, Dennis was invited to attend before the Duke of Northumberland at his home in Alnwick Castle, where he duly presented the salmon to the Duke. This was considered a great honour by the fishing fraternity. The salmon was thereafter taken to the butcher's shop in the village and displayed in the window for everyone to see. In exchange for parting with his catch, Dennis was presented with a beautiful silver trophy to keep for a year and a year's free fishing on the river thereafter. After a year, he would hand the trophy back for the next winner but would receive a smaller cup to keep.

Two months later, when Karen was ten months old, she was sitting in her baby seat and at 6 o'clock there was a knock at the door. This was usual and she got so excited and jumped up and down in her chair, awaiting the arrival of her grandparents whom she knew would make a great fuss of her. However, this was not to be. Ken had answered the door but it was Raymond who stood there. When he came into the room, Pamela knew by his expression that once again he was bringing bad news.

The devastating news was that her dad Dennis had passed away. He had been doing what he loved, fishing for salmon on the river Coquet, when he had collapsed and died at the scene. A fellow fisherman had seen it happen and had immediately gone to help, but there was nothing he could do.

The police had received the news and had been given the task of informing Millicent who was working as usual at the nursery. Thankfully, a sergeant who lived in the same street as the couple had seen the information coming into the station and contacted Raymond Pike who he knew was a close friend. Upon hearing the news, Raymond left work immediately and set off to the nursery.

Millicent of course was used to officers visiting the nursery for one reason or another and when once again they arrived, she said, "Are you here to arrest me?" As they broke the news to her, Raymond appeared behind them and came straight over and immediately gave her the support and care that she needed upon such terrible news. He took her to his home, where Betty was waiting for them. She had prepared a bedroom for Millicent and there she stayed for a few days while coming to terms with the turn of events. Betty catered for visiting relatives and the many friends the couple had, and was such a wonderful friend to Millicent at such a sad time.

The one consolation that brought some comfort to everyone was the fact that he was doing what he loved best when he died. He wasn't at work in a factory, he was outdoors on the river Coquet with his fishing rod in hand in the beautiful setting beneath Warkworth Castle.

The funeral was held at Tynemouth Crematorium and, because it was Easter, by tradition at that time, there were no hymns or music played. Millicent thought it was rather a shame because Dennis had always loved music. The amount of people who were standing outside the building, unable to find room inside, was testament to how well thought of Dennis was to both work colleagues and friends. They had all come to pay their respects to this well liked and well-loved man. Family and friends rallied round and, following the funeral, with the permission of the Duke of Northumberland, a small riverside service was held at Dukes Landing by the pastor from George Angus where he had worked and Dennis' ashes were scattered on the River Coquet. It is believed in folklore that the souls of fishermen soar once again in the form of seagulls and at the very moment of the scattering of the ashes, three seagulls soared over the river, calling out in unison. Could it be? Tommy, Peter and Danny? Who is to say?

As they left the riverbank, an amusing conversation took place between the pastor and Dennis's good friend Clem Clark following the service. "Is the Hermitage nearby?" asked the pastor. Thereafter Clem proceeded to give directions to the men's favourite watering hole in the town, the local pub of that name, as opposed to what the pastor really meant, the historical refuge where a priest in the 18th century lived out his years in isolation on the river. A great deal of laughter followed this exchange, and one that Dennis would have no doubt had a good laugh at too.

Millicent continued to work at the nursery for a further year while she made plans for her future. In less than a year, she had lost both her mother and her beloved husband and felt it was time to leave this family home. She and Dennis had always intended to move back to Scotland when they eventually retired and so, she planned to do exactly that. She would take early retirement, sell up in Newcastle and buy a property in St Abbs or Coldingham.

Clearing the house at Eaglescliffe Drive was no mean feat, bearing in mind that it had been in the family since it was first built in the 1940s. Strangely, just a few months earlier, Dennis had had what Millicent called 'a right good clear out' of the garage, much to her relief because she said it was full to the rafters of all manner of things. Everyone helped pack and clear the contents of the house and then it was placed on the market. Meanwhile, up in Coldingham, The Ministry of Defence who owned property in the village, had decided to sell the officers' houses at what used to be an RAF camp. There were three semi-detached houses and one detached available.

And so, upon the sale of her house in Newcastle, Millicent purchased No 4 Crosslaw and aptly named it Four Winds. This was her new beginning.

Four Winds,
Crosslaw
School Road
Coldingham
Berwickshire
SCOTLAND

Immediate Neighbours:
Celia and Betty Weightman (next door)
Peggy Guy (Tom Kerr's sister)
Mary and Tom Kerr
Nell and George Henderson (former owners
of The Haven at Coldingham Sands)

Mrs Neidveitch – down the path in the detached house.

Down School Road:
Forsythe (Sy) Lindores and his cousin Margaret
Lindores at "Woodbine Cottage"

Nancy and Craig McGuire (across the road from Woodbine Cottage)

Dr Chris and Mrs Marion MacDonald (sons Duncan and Alasdair)
living at "Kirkhill", a large detached house with surrounding
boundary wall of the property and all garden areas, which is on
the left, on the way out of Coldingham towards Eyemouth.

Coldingham Bay
David Cormack – "Dunlaverock"

St Abbs
Jim and Eileen Cormack, Ann and Maureen, at
"Ocean View," the Cormack family home.

Chapter 18

Such a lot of her life, both before and after her marriage to Dennis, had been spent in either St Abbs or Coldingham, so it was actually like home from home. Dennis's brother Jim and his wife Eileen were still living at Ocean View, of course, with their two daughters Ann and Maureen, so it was good to have them close.

Friends Sy Lindores and his cousin Margaret lived down the road in Woodbine Cottage and were always on hand to give a helping hand when needed. Plus her friend Nancy McGuire and her husband Craig lived opposite them. Nancy and Millicent both looked forward to shopping trips together in Berwick!

Next door to her lived Celia and Betty Weightman, who were always out in the gardens, front and back, so whenever Millicent was in her garden, there were always friendly chats over the fence. Whenever the grandchildren came to stay, the Weightmans were extremely kind to them all and made a great fuss of them.

Just a few doors up the road lived Mary and Tom, whom she and Dennis had known for years.

Dr Chris and Marion MacDonald were good friends too and when Pamela was young, they would have her stay for a week each year when both she and their son Alasdair celebrated their birthdays together in June. The couple lived in a large detached house called Kirkhill on the outskirts of Coldingham and it was a house that was visited by all of the Cormack family whenever holidays brought them to the Borders.

Millicent kept herself busy, decorating each room in the house, knocking things down and building things up. It occupied her mind and helped her come to terms with life on her own. It was a struggle at first but over time, she learned to live with the loss of Dennis. The neighbours were always on hand to help whenever she needed it. Sy built a greenhouse and patio in her back garden, so there was somewhere to sit on a sunny afternoon and somewhere to work with her plants when it rained. He also put a roof on the walls around the side of her back door, thus creating a small area protected from the elements.

Village life was good, with plenty of activities organised at the school across the road, dances in the village and surrounding areas, and various places to visit. Millicent soon fell in step with all that went on around her and joined in everything she possibly could.

Mary and Tom would tell Millicent as soon as they got to hear there was a dance up at Haddington, and off they would go. She loved those trips and thoroughly enjoyed the dances. She got to know their nephew too, who lived in the town. He was a police officer and when he heard that Millicent's grandson Craig wanted to be an officer when he grew up, he gave her his old police hat to send on to him. (*A young Craig was thrilled to receive this!*)

For a time, she tried offering 'Bed and Breakfast'. She had spoken with local B & Bs saying that if they were full, rather than send people away they could contact her and she would try and oblige. She did this for a couple of years but found that it was not practical for her, and meant extra work which she could do without.

The family would visit and the grandchildren would often come for holidays. There was always something interesting for them to do, country walks, a choice of beaches to go to and have picnics, with wonderful chip shops and ice cream on offer in Eyemouth, the next town just a short bus ride away. (Sadly not for Susan, though, who was allergic to fish.)

Millicent always managed to make grandchildren's visits both exciting and interesting. There was always something to do and woe betide if anyone was reckless enough to say they were bored! We all remember the shaking of a finger as she said "By the Living Harry' when she had her dander up! It was enough to make you shake in your shoes. (*We all wondered who Harry was, dead or alive!*) No, holidays in Coldingham were never dull.

Over the years, Millicent attended art classes at the school and acquired a definite skill in her paintings. People had started bringing her pictures, asking if she would do a painting to bring it to life for them and Millicent always managed to create exactly what they wanted. It was a helpful source of income as well, although she really just covered what she had to pay for the equipment and paints.

One of her most prolific paintings was one entitled 'Burnham Beeches', a lovely woodland scene with sunlight shining through the branches and catching one branch in particular in brilliant light. It proved so popular, that visitors who had seen it develop, asked her to do one for them too. Her old nursing friend Louise asked her to paint a larger canvas of the scene to give to her husband Alan when celebrating their wedding anniversary. It was magnificent and was later exhibited in a church down in Whitley Bay for all to see. With it being much larger than the normal size paintings, and in that setting, it was breath-taking. Millicent and the family once tried to calculate exactly how many paintings she had done of that scene but had to give up in the end because they lost count!

Millicent used to watch with great interest, a television programme in which an artist called Nancy Kominsky created wonderful paintings, all done with a palette knife. When a competition open to all was announced, Millicent decided to have a go and enter something under the heading 'The Great Outdoors'. She created a mountainous snow scene with skis sticking out of the snow, crossed her fingers and sent it off to the show in London. Amazingly, out of the thousands of entries, hers was among those chosen to be exhibited for the final judging.

She was invited to attend on the day of judging and of course she was thrilled to do just that. Hers was not placed on the day, but she said it had been a great privilege to be part of it and to see all the wonderful paintings that had been entered. She had got to see Nancy Kominsky and Lord Weymouth and be present at the final selection. She had in fact done fantastically well to have got as far as she did in the competition, which had confirmed that she was in fact a very talented artist.

Millicent said she was quite chuffed when she was in the village shop one day and while she was chatting to someone, the woman had suddenly said, "Oh! You're the artist, aren't you?" Praise indeed!

Painting wasn't her only talent, of course. She was also a great knitter of Aran jumpers. She knitted them for every member of the family, extended family, neighbours, friends and friends of friends. She always used the genuine Aran wool which has an oily finish to it which disappears once it is washed.

She made jewellery from polishing stones, and had all the equipment and paraphernalia that went with this. Christmas presents aplenty for the family.

Whatever Millicent put her hand to, the family always seemed to benefit in one way or another (whether you liked them or not!).

Chapter 19

Life in Coldingham village inevitably changed as the years went by. Good friends and family members died, local pastimes became less and the walk up School Road to Four Winds became an increasingly difficult climb for Millicent after shopping in the village. She had suffered from arthritis for years and her knee joint was becoming a painful problem as it was gradually swelling, resulting in an abnormal angle of her lower leg. Walking was awkward and increasingly painful.

Grandchildren were getting older and establishing their own routines and interests so were visiting less and her children were of course all working.

Living on a corner meant that not only did she have a back garden, it wrapped round to the front and met the garden there. Also, there was land across the little access road in front of the house which was all grassed over. This was all becoming a worry and a problem. She was getting older and finding it more difficult to keep on top of the work it required to keep everything neat and tidy. At one point, the family considered buying her a goat to keep on the grassed areas, but that was soon discounted because it would create even more work for her to look after a goat! It did raise a smile though, at the thought of it.

All of these changes brought Millicent to the conclusion that it was time to move back to Newcastle to be near the family and reunite once more with her friends there. She had loved living in a small village, so Pamela and

Alistair were entrusted with the search for a suitable home in a similar community. Wylam was the first choice on her list, but after visiting one property which was an old terraced house that required updating but still quite pricey, they all concluded that it was too expensive there.

One property advertised in a little place called Backworth fired up their interest, and Alistair and Pamela arranged to view it. It was a fairly new and modern semi-detached house, beautifully decorated and with good bus services nearby, and more importantly of all, in a small village-like community. It ticked so many of the boxes of Millicent's preferences, so after discussions and consultations and a small amount of negotiations, an offer was made and accepted. Four Winds had also been advertised and a young couple had loved it immediately and wanted to buy it, so everything was in place for the big move.

It must have been quite emotional for Millicent, saying goodbye to those friends and neighbours in and around Coldingham. Having moved up in 1970, she had lived in the village now for around 14 years, so it really was going to be a wrench, but the right thing to do at this time. It had been a place of peace and quiet after the busy life she had had when she was working and living in Newcastle. She had thrown herself into the village life and had contributed to the community in many ways. Four Winds had provided a happy home with many visitors and family visits but one thing she wouldn't miss was the hard work in the upkeep of the gardens! Thankfully, the new house just had one garden space at the back of the house, which would be much more manageable.

Jimmy Martin from Pilmur Farm offered to move all of the contents of the house down to Newcastle and take Millicent with him, which was wonderful and so typical of the help that villagers offered whenever it was needed.

On the morning of the move, Alistair and Pamela travelled to Backworth, armed with the keys to the property and, after opening up, awaited the arrival of Millicent. They had no idea what sort of vehicle Jimmy would be driving, so when this huge tarpaulin covered wagon came around the corner and rumbled up to the house, they both burst out laughing.

Now around this time, there was a very popular TV show called The Beverley Hillbillies about a poor family called the Clampetts who lived in a run-down shack but when oil was discovered on their land, they moved up in the world. They were rich. Much to the horror of their new neighbours in Beverley Hills, this raggle-taggle family rattled their way into the neighbourhood. Their belongings were piled high on the back of their clapped-out car, and sitting atop all their belongings, sat Granny Clampett on her rocking chair.

The image of the Clampetts' arrival was too near this new image of Jimmy Martin's lorry and Millicent's possessions! All it needed was Millicent to be sitting on top of the tarpaulin to complete the vision! By the time the lorry pulled up in front of the house, the siblings had managed to supress their mirth and greet the new arrivals sensibly.

It was hard work, but between them all, everything was moved into Millicent's new home and after a bite to eat, Jimmy bade farewell and set off to return to Scotland.

She settled in at Backworth and was once again meeting up with her friends, including Lucy and Eppie who lived not far away in Whitley Bay; Betty and Raymond; and Louise, her nursing friend. She joined the local church and got involved with the volunteer work connected to it, which also meant she got to know her neighbours by doing this.

Her love of dancing had not waned and she met up regularly with Lucy and Eppie and they attended a dancing group every week. It was a great social afternoon where everyone joined in happily. Millicent still suffered with arthritis which had gone on for years, but not to be beaten, she applied great amounts of 'Radian B' to her knees or some other pain control cream, rubbed it all well in, and off she would go. They all had a great time at the dance.

Millicent was never idle or bored. There were too many things to do and so many new interests to hold her attention. She was getting older though and, sadly, her physical strength was naturally diminishing and her arthritis was restrictive. She was eventually advised by her doctor to have a knee replacement in an effort to improve her day-to-day living. And later, a hip replacement.

The night before her hip operation, and following a pre-op blood test, the doctors in the hospital discovered too much sugar in her blood and diagnosed her with having diabetes. She was therefore given an insulin injection – which immediately rendered Millicent unconscious. As Millicent later put it, "they were all in a right spin after that, trying to correct the problem". (*Millicent was always of the opinion that the only reason that she had had such an adverse reaction to the insulin injection was the fact that she was not diabetic at all. It just so happened that she had eaten a whopping big chunk of her grandson Iain 's birthday cake the night before, which surely had resulted in the high sugar levels!*) After a group consultation, the medical team agreed that her operation could proceed the following morning as the patient was once again stable.

As the family later came to realise, Millicent used her diabetes to her great advantage as and when it suited her! On weekly outings in the car with Alistair and Edith, if she was getting hungry at all, she would remind them that she would have to eat something soon or she might go into a coma. But on the other hand, diabetes was quickly cast aside if she wanted a tasty looking cream cake, as then it would be a case of 'Well I am only slightly diabetic'. She could be a crafty soul.

After the incident at the hospital, Millicent was devastated to discover that her eyesight had been badly impaired as one of her eyes was not as sharp as it used to be and the other had what she described as a dark shadow over most of it. This resulted later in the sad realisation that she was no longer able to paint her pictures. She did try, but it was no use; her painting days were over. As usual, though, she would not be beaten. There were other crafts to interest her, she just had to discover and decide what.

Christmas morning routines became set in stone as far as Millicent was concerned. Alistair picked her up and she would be practically at the door, coat on, ready for the off. They then travelled to Pamela's, where there would be an exchange of presents while glasses of Bucks Fizz were consumed. The rest of the day was spent with Alistair and Edith at their house. There was no chance that this annual event could or should ever change. Millicent had a way of getting what she wanted.

Boxing Day also became a new arrangement. All the family would meet up at her house, and they brought with them all manner of food and drink to tuck into in a great family get-together. At the end of the afternoon, everyone mucked in, cleared, washed and tidied, and afterwards, after everyone had gone their separate ways, Millicent could sit back and relax. It was always a happy and noisy gathering that reminded her of the days when she was a child at old family gatherings.

During the time Millicent lived in Backworth, many family events happened, birthdays and weddings and a divorce. Susan married Simon and went on to have two daughters, Katie and Emily. Iain went to university at St Andrews and Heriot-Watt, as well as Barcelona to name but a few. Pamela and Ken divorced; Karen met Julian when they both graduated in Lancaster and went on to marry and have two daughters, Tess and Phoebe. Craig had a son, Sam but separated from Sam's mother and daughter Charlotte. He went on to marry Catherine who already had a son called Reece. Pamela met and later married Alan Robson, who also had three sons, Lee, Garry and Craig. The family was expanding, and Millicent thoroughly approved.

Sadly, Millicent was never to meet Iain's wife Barbara or their three girls, Alison, Anna and Ailsa. Oh how she would have so loved to have been able to brag to all and sundry about that pairing. Two clever doctors (didn't matter in what field) meeting, marrying, having children. What a time she would have had! She could brag for England, given half a chance. Never any dull moments in family lives, are there?

For Millicent's 75th birthday, Alistair and Edith took her not so subtle hints that she should do something special to celebrate such a landmark age, and they treated her to a helicopter flight which was to last for at least a couple of hours. They flew down to Whitley Bay – where much to her surprise, she saw Lucy and Eppie waving to her from the promenade on the seafront. They had been forewarned about the trip but much to everyone's amusement, they unknowingly stood above a wall displaying some graffiti stating "Titter ye Not", a well-known saying of Frankie Howerd's (*a comedian/actor*) which seemed to add even more fun to the event. Then it was time to head back to the airport where the pilot did a few tricks to show her what it could do. And Millicent being Millicent, took it all in her stride.

For her 76th the following year, she was again treated by Alistair and Edith. This time they were all going to stay in a hotel called Dunlaverick at Coldingham Sands. This large house had been owned in the past by David Cormack, who was a cousin of Tommy and a retired solicitor. He had been living there when Millicent lived in Coldingham and she always told the funny story of when he had asked her to come for tea one day. Unfortunately, she had to tell him that she wasn't able to come because she had arranged to travel to Newcastle to visit family. She later learned that he gone back to the local bakers where he had purchased a cake for Millicent's visit, handed it over to them and asked for his money back because it wasn't needed. Being a regular customer, how could they refuse! Who would have thought that someone would have the nerve to do that? Things are definitely different in village life.

The house had been sold after David had died and was now run as a small hotel / Bed and Breakfast, and Millicent loved her stay there. The views of Coldingham bay were spectacular and it was a lovely relaxing birthday treat.

She later dropped hints for other birthdays, one of which was a hot air balloon ride. Alistair nipped that right in the bud before the idea even got off the ground. No engines? No wings? NO WAY!

Of course, her impending 80th birthday was something everyone wanted to celebrate. No hints were needed here, although she was heard to have said "A birthday with a nought in it should always be celebrated". So, a surprise party was discussed. It became obvious to everyone that it would make sense to involve Millicent in the planning. It was the only way to make sure the right people were there and no-one was missed out. Plus, it would be nice for her to take part in the organising and give her something definite to look forward to. She made a list of the family, friends and neighbours she would like to be invited and also, what she would like to happen at the do. Bingo and music – and dancing of course.

A local public house called The Deuchers had a lovely big function room and was within walking distance of the village, so it was the ideal venue. There followed a flurry of activity, booking catering, music, bingo callers, and contacting potential guests.

On the morning of the party, the family prepared the room with balloons etc, set the tables and chairs, and got everything ready for the big event.

That night, relatives and friends, old and new, arrived and filled the room. There were a couple of surprises too. Her friends since meeting Dennis, John and Estell Wells, had been invited in secret. Alan and Pamela had booked them into a hotel in Whitley Bay, so they kept out of the way until their arrival at the party. Millicent was taken completely by surprise and absolutely delighted to see them both.

Also there that night was her cousin Olive, and they were to have a conversation which proved invaluable information some years later. Olive told Millicent that she was now living in a home called Sovereign Lodge, in Westerhope, which was quite near to where both Alistair and Pamela lived. She said it was like living in a hotel and she absolutely loved it. She said if you happened to be hungry between your meals, you just had to ask and something would be brought to you. There were regular games of bingo, various craft sessions and other sorts of entertainment occasionally; also a hairdresser came weekly. Millicent liked the sound of all that.

The party was a great success and Millicent was the belle of the ball. Her birthday cake was dished out to everyone and they all went home with some for their supper. She had loved seeing everyone and taking part in the dancing, bingo and of course circulating and chatting with each individual there. Despite her 80 years, she had the energy of someone half her age that night and never flagged. At the end of the night when she was once again in her home and it was all over, she could be forgiven for feeling slightly worn out.

Chapter 20

Millicent's mind was as sharp as a tack but sadly she was not so well physically. She coped with her arthritis and her new limbs but was susceptible to chest infections which could result in spells in hospital and, eventually, she became more and more housebound.

The hospital after-care was very supportive and many aids around the house were installed to make her independent living more possible. A local lady came in to clean for her, and carers called each day to assist her in preparing for bed in the evenings and to rise in the morning and get dressed. This was her way of life for a good few years and she looked forward to her daily visitors, as well as family visits.

In January 2005 when once again Millicent was hospitalised with the usual chest infection and breathing difficulties, she said enough was enough. She did not want to return to her house. She had been thinking about the residential home that she and her cousin Olive had discussed at her birthday party. She told her family, as well as the nursing staff, that she wanted to go where Olive lived. It not only sounded a lovely place, but was also closer to where both Alistair and Edith, and Pamela and Alan lived, in the area west of Newcastle. She told everyone "I have looked after people all my life, I think it's time I was looked after now". And so it came to be.

Her house at Shrewsbury Drive was put on the market and quickly snapped up. The proceeds were required to pay for living at Sovereign

Lodge. It must have been assumed that Millicent's family would object to this, because a meeting between medical staff and people from the council was quickly arranged. They were very surprised when all were seated and the family agreed to their proposals of funding from the house proceeds. It was the law at that time, councils were increasingly short of funds and financially assisted accommodation very limited, so Millicent's family had long accepted that this is what would have to happen. After that, things moved quite quickly and, eventually, Millicent happily joined Olive at Sovereign Court.

She loved it. It gave her a new lease of life.

In recent years, she had not been able to get out and about as often as she used to and became more dependent on her family members to take her out in the car. Trips out for Sunday lunch with some friends had been very welcome but they too had been in decline too. Her close friends were also getting older and less mobile too, so meeting up with them was few and far between. She was used to a busy life and socialising with people, so this quiet life could sometimes be quite lonely for her.

Sovereign Court changed all that. The staff were always busy but friendly and chatty. Everything she needed was in close proximity and she could get about within the home quite nicely. She and Olive would take turns in visiting each other's rooms to have a coffee and a gossip, as well as getting together with the other residents for bingo, and the many other social events organised by the home.

In her private room, she was surrounded by her favourite things, her own paintings, ornaments and of course, photos of her beloved Dennis. It really was a home from home, but on a much smaller scale.

The corridors leading to the dining room, sitting room or other residents' rooms could be quite long, so Alistair purchased a wheeled walker for her. It had four wheels on the framework with handles on the top, and a seat in the centre which lifted up to reveal a basket underneath for storage. This made her journeys much safer and less strenuous. However, Millicent's mischievous side came to the fore when she had a hooter fixed to one of the handles. It had a large rubber bulb and whenever anyone was walking a bit too slow in front of her, or in her way, she would pump the rubber bulb and it parped out a very loud blast. This was really funny but bearing in mind where she was, and considering the age of some of the residents (not to mention their medical conditions) she had to choose carefully when to use it as, obviously, there were sensitive and sometimes grumpy people with heart conditions living there. She had a real twinkle in her eye when she did use it though.

She still loved to be taken out, and Alistair and Edith took her all over in the car. They took her to where she grew up in Carville in Durham and on her 86th birthday they went to Eggleston Hall where she had worked all those years ago for Sir William Gray.

On a Saturday Pamela would take her in the car to Sainsbury's where she would be settled in the café with a cup of coffee while Pamela did her shopping for her. They would have something to eat and then go for a drive around the coastal areas as well as the countryside. This changed, however, when Millicent thought she would prefer to be out on a Sunday because the food at the home was usually a cold buffet, which she was not fond of, so they changed the day and routine.

Therefore, Pamela collected her on her preferred day and they would go for a short run out and afterwards back to her house. Millicent would happily sit in the conservatory and look out into the garden, watching the birds as she always used to in her own home. She would have something to eat and then have a nap while Pamela did the dishes. After that, they would sit and have a chat about lots of things, but mainly about her life with Dennis in the lighthouse service. "Write it all down, Mam," Pamela told her one day. The stories she told were too good to be forgotten and as these chats continued, Pamela herself wrote notes of what Millicent recollected. Millicent later gave her a red exercise book in which she had been putting down her thoughts and it really made engrossing reading.

As usual she had a hobby, this time making greetings cards, Easter, Christmas and Birthday cards. She made them to send to friends and family, as well as making them to order for the residents. One particular carer, Michael, took craft lessons regularly and she would always involve herself in whatever he demonstrated. One time, when she was given a bag full of bright and sparkly bottles of nail varnish, she handed them over to Michael who was happy to oblige and paint the ladies' nails. Those who wanted to participate, happily went back to their rooms with very attractive hands!

In January 2007, residents and staff were preparing for a Burns Night supper to be held on 25th January. This was one of Millicent's favourite nights. Having been married to a Scot, it was a traditionally celebrated event in which she had participated on many occasions. She asked Pamela if she could bring a tartan rug up to the home, for use in the celebration and when she called in with the rug on her way home, Pamela was concerned that Millicent looked not quite right. It transpired that she had been at a game of bingo that afternoon and the outside door had been left open where they had all been sitting, and she had felt really cold. She still felt chilled, despite being wrapped up, but was sure she would be fine and was pleased she had the rug for Burns Night. The following morning, it was evident that the chill had turned into something far more serious and an ambulance had been called. She was taken to Newcastle General Hospital and she was not happy. She kept saying to Pamela that she hoped she would be out in time for Burns Night as she didn't want to miss it. She did love a party.

The news that Millicent then developed pneumonia was devastating to the family. They were all aware of how fragile she was these days and such an illness was extremely worrying. She was transferred to the Freeman Hospital, where a few days later, sadly, Millicent lost her fight for life. She was 89.

But it had been a good life. A life full of children, family, laughter and adventure.

She had not lost one iota of her spirit either.

While she was terribly ill in the hospital, one of the nurses had cheerfully called her Millie, and as anyone who knew her and would expect of her, the nurse was very quickly reprimanded and told:

"It's not Millie, its Millicent!"

At Millicent's funeral, a tape of children singing was played, and a recording of Be Nobody's Darling but Mine.

A few days later, the family once again returned to Dukes Landing on the river Coquet, and in the shadow of Warkworth Castle, her ashes were scattered at the same place as Dennis' had been all those years ago. It was a beautiful day, calm and sunny and a great feeling of peace was felt by them all. The thistle and the rose were reunited once again.

The couple had had a wonderful life together, filled with laughter, fun and adventure. When Dennis died, Millicent filled her life with family, friends and new challenges, and all in all, she rose to whatever challenges she faced. It had been a busy life. A hard-working life.

It was also a life well lived.

OUR TRIP TO INCHKEITH

In 2018 I wrote to Sir Tom Farmer (who was the founder of the Kwik Fit tyre company and the owner of Inchkeith Island). I had learned that if you wanted to visit there, you had to obtain his permission first.

I therefore wrote and explained that my parents had lived there during the war, where my father was a lighthouse keeper and as I dearly wished to visit there, could he find his way to allow this? Around two weeks later, I received a telephone call directly from him. To say I was shocked would be an understatement and that's a fact. I stuttered and stammered at first, trying to gain control of my thinking, and said I was really touched that he had actually rang me personally. He happily told me about some of his home life, the fact that he had been the sixth and youngest child in the family and therefore totally spoilt. He asked me a bit more about my visit to the island and what I planned to do, which I duly did. I also asked if it would be OK for my daughter, son and husband to come with me as well.

He confirmed that he was indeed happy for us all to go, but stipulated that we must have personal insurance in place because the island was now quite dangerous because of all the derelict buildings, potholes etc.

We chose a date to go in August and emailed confirmation of everyone's insurance certificate to Sir Tom's office. They were very helpful in recommending 'a man with a boat' who I could contact, which I managed to do and booked him immediately.

So, Alan, Karen, Craig, Catherine and I stayed overnight at our caravan in Eyemouth and on the following morning, the 15th August, four of us set off for Edinburgh. Catherine had volunteered to stay and look after Jock – as well as prepare a meal for us when we came back later that day, which was a great help.

After a short stop off for breakfast in Edinburgh, we drove up to Granton Harbour where we were to meet Bill Simpson, the owner of the 'Conserver', who would take us across. We all had to climb down the ladders set in the harbour wall to get aboard the boat which was a real physical challenge. Plus, the lower section was very rusty as a result of being submerged every time the tide came in. Not to mention the fact that it was a long way down!

The journey over there was luckily fine, no strong swells to upset our stomachs. As we got nearer to the island, the lighthouse was gradually coming into view right on the very top. We turned into the shelter of the jetty, which was a great long structure leading to the small beach there. We then had to disembark – by hauling ourselves up another set of ladders set in the jetty wall, in an even worse condition than those in Granton. Some of the brackets fixing them to the wall were missing, or hanging loose, and the rust was much more evident. It would have given those concerned with health and safety at work a real headache!

We all took lots of photos that day. There were old look-out towers, many, many derelict buildings which had been used by the Forces living there (which we had to shelter in at first because the heavens opened). Then came the walk up Heartbreak Hill, which made me think 'poor Mam', having this to climb when she was pregnant each time she returned from the mainland. When we reached the top of the bank, the path veered left, past some more derelict houses, and then as we turned the corner, there before us was a large paved area, with the lighthouse at the far end ahead. To our right were even more derelict houses.

The lighthouse buildings themselves were the only ones that were in a good order. The tower and the adjoining living quarters were painted in the standard tonal cream colours and were clean and tidy. The Northern Lighthouse Board have automated all lighthouses, including Inchkeith, but they continue to maintain the interior workings, and the exterior of the tower and the lighthouse buildings.

We opened a little bottle of champagne there in front of my parents' first home together, and raised our glasses in a toast to them both. It was quite a moving and memorable moment.

Everywhere else on the island was in a dreadful state of decay. From a drawing that my mother had done in an exercise book, we could work out where she lived, where her wash room was, and the green to dry the washing, as well as where the military officers lived. Their houses stood to the right of the lighthouse, facing the open flagged area where the rest of the soldiers' and sailors' accommodation had once stood. There wasn't much left of the roofs, and most of the floorboards inside had disintegrated, but inside one house, a fireplace and range were still in place.

There were also, sadly, many dead and dying birds. There had been an outbreak of a particularly evil virus and they were paying the price for scavenging for food where the disease was rife.

We all walked to the east of the island where the huge cannons used to be housed. The pits and surrounding structures were very much intact and were amazing to see. There were lookout shelters all over too, facing in all directions. Most were too dangerous to go anywhere near, as they were crumbling away and overgrown with weeds and grass.

It was an incredible experience walking around the island that day and trying to imagine what it must have been like in war time, when soldiers and sailors were on lookout duty for enemy aircraft and to protect the entrance to the River Forth, the bridges and Edinburgh itself. Enemy submarines were known to risk a chance up the river too.

When we had viewed as much of the place as we could, we made our way down the hill to the bay below. We found somewhere to sit and tucked into the food and refreshments we had brought. Eventually we walked onto the jetty and looked over to Leith to see if we could see the 'Conserver' to come back and take us once again to the harbour in Granton.

From the jetty wall, thankfully, we could see the boat in the distance, gradually making its way towards us.

When Bill steered the boat into the bay, we walked along the long narrow jetty and once again tackled the challenge of climbing down those rusty ladders to the boat. It was strong in our mind that we also had to climb up the other set of ladders when we got back to Granton, but no-one wanted to say so.

It was a tired foursome who travelled back to Eyemouth and it was lovely to get back to the caravan to relax. Mindful of the disease that existed on the island, we doused all our shoes in disinfectant and left them outside for a few hours. Catherine had made a delicious sausage casserole, and boy, did we all enjoy eating that. Scrumptious!

I wanted Sir Tom to know that we had really appreciated being able to do what we did, so I wrote another letter to him, thanking him once more and copied two photos on the letter. One of us setting off in the morning, and one of my parents when they got engaged and Dad was in his lighthouse uniform.

I thought that would finalise things nicely. However, I was surprised and very touched to receive yet another letter from him saying how pleased he was that we would always have pleasant memories of our trip.

It had been like a step back into the past, and a step into my parents' lives which I could never have experienced, had we not walked on Inchkeith Island.

Pamela Doreen Robson